LINES OF THUNDER

The First Days on the Front

WALTER BLAIRE

Edited by
KATE LECHLER

ISBN: 978-0-9978146-1-3

TIMELINE OF BOOKS

The books of the Haphanverse have overlapping characters and events, but they can be read as standalones or in a series. This timeline puts the books in the real chronology. The years count from Landing Day, when the Haphan Empire arrived to colonize planet Gregory IV:

- Year 51: First year of the trench war
- Year 141: **What the Thunder Said** (novel)
- Year 142: **The Shaping Trip** (story)
- Year 145: **By Mirth Exceeded** (in 2019)
- Year 150: *Lines of Thunder* ← this book
- Year 156: **The Eternal Front** (novel)

For my children

CONTENTS

❈ I ❈

THE FIRST DAY

❧ I ❧

---

*In which Gole Naremsa, private in the 51st Fusiliers, makes a
new enemy on his first day on the eternal front.*

GOLE WAS DROWSING IN A PILE OF SLEEPING SOLDIERS AND
only half aware when the troop train shuddered to a stop.

They'd been cooking for a day and a half in the window-
less carriage, breathing each other's air and staring at the
sliver of light around the sliding door. Earlier, when the sun
was at its peak, they'd been sure they would suffocate. They
tried to wrench the door open but it was heavy wood, banded
with iron, utterly impervious. At the cost of several broken
fingers they only added more pitiful scratches to the inside
surface.

The carriage had no benches, which didn't matter: They
were so many they only had room to stand. Later, when their
legs gave out, they discovered they could sleep in piles like
the dead.

The train gave a final jolt and the door slid open. The carriage flooded with blinding late-day sunlight.

"No more sleeping, ye scrags," someone shouted.

They tried to unravel themselves but they weren't fast enough. The bright square of the doorway filled with figures. Gole blinked at them. The newcomers were soldiers, but these were lean and filthy, with torn uniforms. They weren't new replacements like Gole, they were actual *boots,* the soldiers who fought the eternal front. They began tossing people bodily out of the train.

"It's a mess, la, if the Southies barrage the train," the voice continued. "So make all due haste."

A pair of hands grasped Gole's jacket and lifted him out of the sweaty, exhausted soup of men. Gole complicated matters by latching onto his twin brother, who was buried beside him. Grulle immediately clasped back with an iron grip. They were not going to be separated. The debarking lost its brisk rhythm.

"What delay?" the voice snapped.

"They're sticking together, la," said Gole's handler.

"He's my blood-fed brother," Gole tried to explain. His tongue was so dry and swelled he barely understood his own words.

"Corphy, this one says he's a bother," the man relayed over his shoulder.

Laughter from the other boots.

Then the strap on someone's pack snapped apart, freeing Gole's leg, and he popped out of the pile. They slung Gole and Grulle through the door and into the waiting arms of—

No one. They hit the ground. Gole's Tachba reflexes finally activated and he rolled to his feet. Grulle landed upright, making him look clumsy in comparison, as always.

The eternal front at last.

On shaky legs, Gole turned to take it in, screwing his eyes

against the light. Not much to see at first. His new world seemed to mostly consist of young replacements who were already covered in dust and trying to get their legs back. Distinctly prosaic, not glorious at all.

In the distance, however, shimmering in the hot air, were some of the big beasts he'd heard about in stories. Gole's eyes fastened on them and he momentarily forgot everything else.

The machines were over twelve feet tall but they looked like men hunched under a burden. They weren't alive, but if the stories were true they could *seem* alive. They went where they were told and did as they were bid. The Haphan Overlords controlled them, called them *bots*. If the South ever overran the reserve trench, these beasts were the defense of last resort. What Gole didn't expect were the long square blades that fanned from the upper limbs. Three blades per side, each covered in dirt and longer than a grown man.

"They look more like locomotives, don't they?" Gole said, pointing. "Not scary at all."

Grulle started to look—but then lurched forward and collapsed to the ground. He'd been hit from behind.

Gole's Tachba reflexes took over before Grulle stopped sliding. He pivoted on his heel and flung out a fist. Even without looking, his backhand connected with his brother's assailant. A childhood of training, the way Grulle had fallen, *and the Pollution*—Gole knew precisely where the other's center of mass would be.

The other man was a Tachba too, however, and already dodging. Gole's backhand was a glancing blow, eliciting only a soft grunt—but now Gole had the man's height and weight. This one was big and solid. A full adult.

The Pollution shivered in Gole's mind, an unwholesome spurt of pleasure at the challenge presented by this unexpected enemy. *Full grown,* the Pollution seemed to whisper. *Experienced. Habit-ridden.*

The Pollution tried to turn him toward the enemy but that would be exactly what the man expected. Gole fought the compulsion, and instead spun the other direction, momentarily turning his back. *Never, never!* the Pollution howled. But the unusual move let Gole strike from a surprising direction.

He landed a roundhouse in the middle of the man's face.

Gole himself was not big and solid, but the punch stopped the man dead. He teetered, giving every impression of astonishment that he'd been clocked by a raw youth. He'd been unprepared for Gole's follow-up, or really for anything from Gole. He even held an open canteen in one hand, as if he'd taken a drink before he hit Grulle and started everything.

Gole plucked the canteen out of the man's hand and watched him sit on the ground. He landed hard.

"Stay down," Gole said. "This is over."

He took a deep draught and the water unclenched his throat. When he lowered the canteen, he found it wasn't over.

The man was back on his feet, grinning like a maniac. Gole could guess what his Pollution was telling him, and it wasn't favorable. Even worse, with a longer look, Gole could also see something he'd missed before: a small, mud-colored patch on the man's dirty green collar.

Gole had just knocked over a sergeant.

Striking a superior! It wasn't done. His Pollution turned off like a switch.

"Let's call it even," Gole suggested.

He had just enough time to toss the canteen to Grulle before the sergeant's fist eclipsed his vision. The rest of the fight was more predictable than the beginning. Size and experience made trivial work of everything Gole tried.

GOLE'S NEW ENEMY TURNED OUT NOT TO BE THE RAVENING horde of primitive southerners filling the trenches only a hundred yards away—though they probably didn't like him either. It was the noncommissioned officer of his own unit.

"Typical luck," Gole said, through cracked and bloodied lips.

"Very typical," his twin brother mumbled. "Not worth the fight."

Grulle was essentially mute except around family. For a moment, Gole forgot his anger and simply marveled that Grulle had spoken aloud while surrounded by strangers.

"He knocked you over for no reason," Gole said, then grinned. "That's *my* job. Of course I had to fight him."

Grulle shook his head and looked away, unamused. Grulle's profile always bothered Gole, and not just because it was his own. Seeing it every minute of the day made it impossible to escape himself. He invariably noticed how *almost* normal they looked: the sharp jaws, the heavy eyebrows over blue-green eyes, the unruly thick black hair. All of it was promisingly average, but the features somehow didn't mesh.

Grulle also lacked Gole's wrinkles around his eyes and across his forehead, the lines that came from thinking and worrying. Grulle was the blood-fed twin; he never frowned and rarely smiled. All the troubles of the world accumulated on Gole alone. They were finally old enough that Grulle had started to look younger than him.

Grulle noticed him staring and added, "You *are* an angry little scrag."

"I'm friendly but challenging."

Grulle rolled his eyes expressively.

"So you're a chatterbox, now?" Gole snapped. "I guess that means you're scared."

Grulle only answered by shifting his gaze again. Beside the staging area where they had mustered was the black, damp bulk of the earthworks. It was the edge of the empire. The beginning of the trench system that would bring Gole and his brother into the eternal front.

Gole hadn't noticed the earthworks earlier. He hadn't had the chance, distracted first by the bots and then the significantly one-sided episode with the sergeant. Now, it dominated his vision. They were well and truly at the front.

This is the real war, he thought.

For a moment, foreboding thrilled through his body—in the very meat and bones that knit him to existence. A surge of animal fear that nearly washed rational thought from his head.

The fear immediately dissipated, as he knew it would, replaced by a warm, competent excitement. The overlaid emotion felt alien in his mind, a saccharine flavor that didn't taste right for several long seconds. For once, he was grateful for the wrongness. He leaned into the Pollution and accepted its clumsy substitutions. Still, his people's genetic tampering would be easier to accept if he didn't have to notice it every time.

This is our new world. This grime, noise, and stultified air would be their existence from now on. It should have been exciting. It was, finally, the start of his real life. He'd trained for this war since the age of five, and he was finally about to feed himself into the insatiable trenches, one soldier among millions. So why did all of this feel wrong in its core? Why was he resisting it, turning irritable, and shooting his mouth off?

Why had he punched the sergeant and gotten himself beaten to a pulp?

The soldier next to Gole elbowed him. "The lieutenant, and pass the word."

Gole glanced at his twin, knew Grulle wouldn't pass anything if he could help it, and told the next soldier down the line.

Alert now, the replacements saw the lieutenant when he appeared: a handsome, squared off officer with brown thatch hair, a deep front line tan, and heavily patched trench gear. He was making his way through the chaos of the staging area where the fresh replacements had marshaled to meet their officers.

Sergeant Corphy took his place in front of the formation and braced with his arms behind his back. He was a big man with a face set in a permanent sneer. Gole had only landed that first punch on it, to his regret. As the lieutenant walked up, Corphy cleared his throat and addressed them.

"You useless scrags," he shouted, and shot Gole an acid look. "You're only good for dying. You stop a bullet before it hits a real soldier, then you're worth what we paid your mommas. La, you'll die like a pile of corroaches in the rain. Welcome to the 51st Ville Emsa Fusiliers, I hate all of you."

Gole waited for more, but no, the sergeant only had that one message. Corphy turned to salute the lieutenant, but spun back.

"Who laughed?"

"That was me," Gole said. "I'm sorry, sergeant, I thought you were going a different direction with that."

"What's with the squeaker, Corphy?" the lieutenant said. His tone was mild and invited a direct answer.

Gole opened his mouth, but Grulle slammed a fist into his ribs, behind his arm, where neither the noncom nor the officer would have to acknowledge it. Gole emitted only a whistle at the edge of hearing.

"Some talky scrag which don't know he's dead yet," the sergeant answered. "Wanted a fight first thing off the train. Now he dislikes my welcoming speech."

"The one that goes, 'you're all going to die?'" The lieutenant had a ready smile, which he turned on the replacements. "My name is Lieutenant Panthan Elyseuran, and that's the only name you need to know." He jerked his thumb at the towering earthworks, which loomed like a dark future behind his head. "When you walk in there, that's the end for you. Maybe you expected Sergeant Corphy to tell you some tricks for staying alive. Don't even try to stay alive. If you live through today, you might learn a little, but you'll die tomorrow. If you live through tomorrow, you'll learn a little more, but you'll die the day after that. And so on, and so forth, *et cetera,* for days and weeks and months and years. You will never have love, nor family, nor hope ever again. Learn that now and you won't be a burden to your fellow boots."

"Sir, then why speak to us at all?" Gole said.

The lieutenant didn't answer directly. He turned back to the sergeant, who said, "He's the one in this batch, I expect."

In Gole's peripheral vision, Grulle slumped.

"My name is Golephan Naremsa, sir," Gole said.

"Wrong," the sergeant snapped, "you don't have a name. You just wasted three seconds of everybody's life, drawing attention to yourself. Do any of you scrags disagree with me on this point?"

None of the other soldiers indicated disagreement, which Gole accepted equably.

"I'm wasting time on you because it's expected of the officers," the lieutenant said. He tipped his head at the parade stand, the platform on timber stilts that rose thirty feet above the staging area. On it, a collection of officers in clean gray uniforms watched the proceedings.

The Haphans. This was Gole's first look at the overlords, the ones who had subjugated half the planet and ran the war. The overlords for whom Gole and Grulle had been brought into service, and for whom they would probably die.

They looked small.

Small like twelve-year old children, only five or six feet tall. They were fully as human as the Tachba, but they lacked the height, the heft, and the speed. Their very cleanliness above the mud made them seem insubstantial, as if they'd been painted onto the real world. Which, Gole supposed, they had. Over a hundred years earlier, they'd landed in ark ships from space. Using advanced technology and fabulous weapons, they had dominated the native race of gene-twisted Tachba for their own safety. When they could expand no further, they sent their servitor Tachba to fight against the free, unconquered Tachba of the South.

Gole turned away from the Haphans and noticed the lieutenant's gaze on his face. The officer had collected Gole's general lack of admiration for the Haphans and now wore a straight-lipped smile that only reached his eyes.

"So by all means," the lieutenant said in general, but, Gole felt, for him specifically, "stick out in all your unique specialness. The rest of us will think about snipers and take cover behind you."

Gole started to reply, but Grulle punched him again.

The lieutenant's eyes shifted to Grulle. "Thank you for your initiative, soldier. Are you his blood-fed twin?"

Grulle stared back impassively, which was the only answer the lieutenant needed. The lieutenant nodded, then suddenly shook his head, exasperated. "And that's how it starts. See how insidious it is? One mouthy squeaker has a blood-fed twin. I've learned another piece of information which will do me no good. I should be sleeping, la. I've been here a good two minutes, enough to satisfy those..."

He didn't bother to finish. He spun on his heel and stalked back to the trenches.

So there's my life, Gole thought bleakly. *A childhood spent fighting the Pollution to become a useful, high-function part of the war. Yet all the while, I was already as good as dead? And all in the service of—*Gole took another look at the Haphan officers, elevated above the field of Tachba replacements—*of them.*

❧ 3 ❧

GOLE KEPT HIS MOUTH DILIGENTLY SHUT DURING THE march into the trenches. He remembered exactly none of the twists and turns. Every inch of it was identical in its dust, decay, and disorganization. By the end of the trek Gole had seen not a single thing that looked new. From the shovels to the sandbag walls to the soldiers themselves, everything looked to have been repaired a dozen times and then abandoned.

He and Grulle were directed to a nondescript length of trench and ordered to wait. More tired than he expected, Gole slid down the wall into a squat.

Grulle was nervous in this desolate place. "Get the skin, brother."

Gole didn't want to move, but it comforted Grulle to see that he still had it. From his breast pocket, he pulled out a round scrap of leather and shook it open. It had tooth marks around the edges, meaningful to them both. The years had made it soft and pliant, but it still bore the sigil of their family. The tattoo had been made by the shaky, inexpert hand of a little girl, their sister Nana. The skin always made them think of home, and for a long moment they forgot all about the trench.

"So, la, you're the trouble-maker!" Gole glanced up and saw an older soldier easing down next to him. He shoved the skin sigil back inside his coat. The soldier added, "Which I'm called Amalon Mallonemsa."

"I was just told that we don't have names," Gole said.

"I have several, to be sure," the man grinned. "Call me Malley."

Gole introduced himself and his brother.

"I'm guessing you met Sergeant Corphy and ate his welcoming speech," Malley said. "Don't believe him for a second. We all have names."

"So we're not going to die first thing?"

Gole had an edge of sarcasm, which Malley overlooked. "Oh, you'll die, all right. Don't be too angry at Corphy in your head. In his way he's doing you a kindness. You'll be more settled when you get plinked."

"You people at the front are funnier than anybody gives you credit for," Gole muttered.

"Na-na-*not* funny," Grulle blurted, too loud. Gole and Malley turned to him, took in the quivering O of his mouth, the anxiety in his eyes.

Malley put up a hand to block Grulle's gaze. "Don't let him look at you with those. He's close-looking. It's Pretty Polly flirting with him, the Pollution. Nothing good comes of it."

Gole simply stared, mystified and a little guilty. When Grulle shifted his blank stare up the trench, Malley leaned forward and swung his fist. It was so casual and unhurried that Gole didn't even think to react. Malley's fist connected with Grulle's chin, snapped his head around. Grulle winced, blinked away tears, and held his jaw.

"You feel confusion bubble up in you like a piss you can't

hold back, that's the Pollution trying to clear your mind before a fight. It never picks the right time."

"I've been afraid before—" Gole started.

"You don't know what this is," Malley said. "This is Pretty Polly, she's the Pollution for the real war. This is from the beasts what gave us our first twisting. They wanted us to sit quietly and pay attention before going into action. Old servitor controls. Just punch the chin if you see a man go stupid."

"I'll be punching all day, I guess."

Malley fixed him with an even stare. "Word is that you can't shut up."

"Never does, la," Grulle muttered.

"Should I be scared and nervous like Grulle?" Gole asked, honestly curious. He searched inside himself but felt nothing. His earlier anxiety was gone.

"If you had a clue, you would be. But it's different for the smart twin, sometimes. No offense," Malley added to Grulle.

"Where's yours?" Gole asked.

"My brother? Dead." Malley's tone was flat. "Look around, scrag. Most of us are singletons now. If you two think you'll die together, put that thought behind you. Sooner or later, one of you will be without the other."

Gole traded glances with Grulle, who seemed slightly cheered by the idea.

A whistle sounded up the trench: *muster here*. Corphy jogged past, reeling off orders to some following corporals who split away to harangue the men.

"What's happening?" Gole asked.

"We're going over." Malley climbed to his feet. "Give yourself a chance today, scrag. Don't stick out."

"Going over?"

"Going over the bags. The *sand* bags." Malley finally showed a touch of exasperation. He pointed to the top of the trench two feet above their heads. "We're climbing into the air for a patrol. We're hunting Southies. The Southerners." He paused when Gole still didn't answer. "Surely you've heard we have an *enemy?*"

The whistle sounded again. Grulle shrugged at Gole and followed Malley down the trench.

IT WAS A REGULAR PATROL. CORPHY CALLED IT A *GAWK*. They were to climb out of the trenches and muck around in the open. It was just the platoon, nothing big like an assault or a push. Any southerners they found should be treated harshly and sent back either to their lines or to their ancestors.

Gole tried to follow all the new terms—the gawk, how much *lug* they'd carry in their *kit*, the *powter* used for *blacking*, the *sootfat* they added to powter at night to *slighten the cheek-shine, la*. Growing up, he and his brothers had thought they'd mastered trench talk, but this, like everything else, was the real version. As the soldiers listened to Corphy they painted their faces with blacking.

Gole felt it then. The strangeness of this new world landed on his shoulders like a loose sand-bag. The tightness of his chest made breathing difficult. He noticed Grulle studying him, preparing a fist for his chin with a little too much readiness. He tried to control his emotion, but this trench—he'd never seen anything like it. It wasn't just one trench facing the South. It was a whole infrastructure. It had required an hour at a brisk pace to get from the staging area to the dangerous edge. In his first day, Gole had already seen more half-buried pathways and avenues than a fair-sized city.

Three feet south of Gole was the end of civilization. The Haphan Overlords controlled everything until this trench, but past it, no more empire. Beyond the trench was a dark, unknown land full of regressive, violent members of his race who had never felt the Haphan leash or known true civilization. This world with all its detail and potentially life-saving lore, so little of which Gole knew: *This* was his new existence.

"La, drop kit and lighten lug, and pass the word."

The soldiers unbuckled their belts and satchels, leaving them in piles on the trench floor. Gole and Grulle did the same with their full backpacks.

A ladder came up the trench, maneuvered carefully through the traverses—the angles in the trench. To Gole the ladder looked like work, considering they could scramble up the sandbags without it. But there was probably something to be said for moving quietly and paying attention to the world beyond.

"Pass the word, silence discipline."

No talking.

The ladder—more a ramp with wooden slats than a ladder with rungs—was set against the trench parapet and braced against the far wall.

A soldier climbed onto it and walked up in a crouch. Though his face was blacked and obscured, Gole recognized him as Malley from the particular rips and repairs of his coat. He climbed, and as his head grew level with the top of the trench, his rhythm changed. It was no longer a bipedal, rocking rhythm, but something slippery and odd in the air. This was a Tachba walking into danger, and the ancient Pollution subtly changed his bearing to make him harder to pick out. It synched his movements to the wafting smoke and dust of the front.

Malley cleared the trench and disappeared from view.

No gunfire. It was quiet and stayed quiet.

The next soldier climbed the ladder and disappeared with similar promising ease.

Corphy waved a hand and made a series of gestures in hand-sign: "Now the idiot goes up."

Gole guessed the sergeant meant him. He put a foot on the ladder and found that it held his weight.

Of course it held his weight. Why wouldn't it? *I'm wasting time*.

He forced himself up the steps.

He felt drunk, like he was made entirely of feet. He lurched higher, the trench floor sinking below him. The painted faces of the soldiers watched with interest to see if he'd be the first plinked.

Shit, shit, shit...

If his Pollution was taking over, changing his gait and camouflaging his motions, he didn't feel it. He tried not to let himself dwell. He knew he had the knack from hunting as a child, and it wasn't something that could be called when it was wanted. Nothing about the Pollution could be called when wanted, and usually nothing was wanted at all.

Gole cleared the parapet of the trench and glanced back. Corphy seemed disappointed, but waved the next soldier up. Gole turned to face the world above the trench.

4

CRAP!

Gole stepped on someone's leg. It rolled under Gole's boot in a way that had to be painful. The idiot had chosen to lie right in front of the ladder. The soldier was difficult to see and half-buried in the ground.

Gole overcompensated with his next step, placed his foot on a pile of dirt that collapsed, and finally fell on his ass, right onto the hidden soldier's back. Air hissed through the soldier's mouth, a yelp that broke the general silence.

"Your pardon," Gole said, automatically.

Two hands grasped his shoulders and pulled him flat.

"Shut the mouth-hole, ye fucking lunatic," Corphy hissed in his ear.

"But the—" Gole remembered the silence discipline, and finished in hand sign. "A friend below."

"It's a corpse, you blithering—"

Hand sign wasn't a Haphan invention. It was the old hunting language of the Tachba, used when silence mattered, and it dated from before the Haphan Landing. It was rich with profanity, and Corphy let him have it for at least a full minute as more soldiers streamed up the ladder and into the open.

Gole and Corphy both laid across the body, mashing it deeper into the soft earth. Gole looked closely and yes, the man was dead, less than a week so. Skin stretched over bones, eyes sunk and infested with larval oar beetles. That yelp that Gole had elicited when he sat—it was simply air from the lungs, jetting through vocal cords that weren't yet too corrupted to work. This man had just been left up in the open, in the air. Anybody could have safely dragged him into the trench and sent him back for burial.

"—So stop dicking around with Yaelaphan's dead body," Corphy finished. It was amazing how so much irritation could be communicated without voice. "Stop calling attention to yourself. Stop confusing the other new scrags. If I hear another sound out of you, squeaker, I'll pull a summary on you and bullet your brain."

Gole formulated an argument against the justice of that, but Corphy had an actual pistol in his hand, and the pistol was resting on Gole's shoulder with the muzzle toward his chin.

Gole satisfied himself with nodding.

Corphy crawled forward, and Gole turned to follow.

But when he shifted off the corpse—off Yaelaphan—the deformed rib-cage righted itself. Air sucked through Yaelaphan's lips with a long, slobbering sob.

Corphy spun back, face red, veins bulging in his forehead. His pistol angled toward Gole.

Another soldier landed on Yaelaphan. The corpse exclaimed again, a word like, "Mawp!"

"Sorry, sarnt," the soldier signed. "Sorry, Yaelli."

Corphy hesitated, his face ticking as he wavered between what the Pollution wanted and what was wise. At last he turned away, and the pistol disappeared back inside his jacket.

The soldier winked at Gole and crawled forward.

The next soldier up the ladder made a full detour to bounce once on Yaelaphan's back, "Ssfwaa!" He gave it a friendly slap on the head and scrambled away.

Grulle finally appeared over the parapet and immediately noticed Yaelaphan's corpse. He shook his head and circumvented the dead man, stepping on Gole himself before following the rest of the platoon.

Gole calmed his mind as much as possible and crept after his brother. Though he'd been among the first to climb up, he was now behind the main body of men. He spotted the smiling lieutenant, Elyseuran himself, bellying along the dirt just below the lips of a series of shell holes. Grulle was shadowing the lieutenant, which seemed wise, so Gole did the same. If they stuck close to the officer, they'd never officially become separated from the platoon.

For the next hour, Gole's world shrank to the twenty inches of dirt in front of his face, and the wriggling soles of Grulle's boots near the top of his vision. The ground was soft, pliant, and full of curious trinkets that caught his eye. Cracked old bones, empty casings, buttons, scraps of fabric. The dirt was luxuriously soft and his hands sank into it without effort. It had been turned into loose, moist soup from the endless artillery barrages of the front, and he only kept afloat by lying flat and spreading his weight.

Occasionally, a shell hole would yawn under his chin and he'd scramble back before he slid into the pit. The newest holes had smooth steep walls just waiting to avalanche into the brackish water at the bottom. The preferable pits, the ones where Lieutenant Elyseuran paused to take reports from other soldiers scouting ahead, were older and packed to firmness by rain and time.

Movement was backbreaking labor. It was all slithering; even hand-and-knee crawling would have been a relief. Yet they could not have gone faster if they stood up. There were places where men simply dropped into the earth and had to be fished out by their heels.

"Malley call 'em mumblety dirt, la," Grulle whispered, during a brief rest.

"Quiet discipline," Gole signed.

"We'em not quiet now," Grulle replied, gesturing around.

The South had commenced an artillery barrage, and shells were falling on the trenches behind them. The Haphan artillery woke up and answered. Shells crossed the sky with the sound of tearing paper. The explosions were muffled *whumps,* distant, which still somehow thrummed through Gole's body and changed his balance. Silence discipline had relaxed as the noise mounted, and Grulle wasn't the only one whispering aloud.

Gole turned back to his blood-fed. Grulle was breathing hard, covered in blacking and grime, and pouring sweat. But he was also grinning with excitement, another emotion Gole didn't presently share. Grulle seemed more at home in the no-man's-land between the trenches than some of the older soldiers.

"How far to the southern trench?" Gole asked the man next to them.

"How would I know?"

"Well, it's been an hour, so...?"

"Which we don't crawl a straight line," the soldier said. "The Southies are only a hundred yards from home trench. It's not hard to find them. We're simply following some tape laid out by the scouts to keep us clear of bogs and minefields. We stumble across some enemy, we roll them up. That's all you need to know."

"Surely. Why would I need to know more than that?" Gole muttered.

The soldier, who had turned away, pivoted back with a hard stare. "Was that *sarcasm?*"

Gole nodded cautiously.

"I *like* that. That was nice. I can't do sarcasm, meh. Pretty Polly stole it off me with a kiss." His grin was startlingly bright with his other features blacked out.

"I'm sorry for that?" Gole tried.

"I got things in trade," the soldier shrugged. He leaned back and gave a bone-cracking stretch. "Call me Dephic, which it's mostly my name. Now let's see, you said you wanted other things to know about the front? I can unfold that far. Don't salute the officers—I saw your hand twitch when Lieutenant Elyseuran spoke to you. If you salute, it tells the snipers who to plink. Better damn believe you're in the scope right now, being studied like an oar beetle studies a fresh corpse. Your uniform is too clean, shows you're new, prone to make mistakes. You salute, or nod too obsequious-like, and that's the end of our lieutenant. You follow?"

Gole nodded, but not obsequiously.

"Then what else? Ah, I saw you bouncing on Yaelaphan's corpse. You could avoid that in the future. Also, don't drink your water too quickly. And if comes to a pinch, let your blood-fed do your fighting. They're better at it than you are, ego be damned."

Gole glanced at Grulle, who nodded sagely.

"And the last thing," Dephic added, "don't get shot by Corphy. You'd think this would go without saying. I saw him draw his pistol on you, and frankly, I'm surprised you're still scragging through the mumblety."

"Corphy really *shoot* idiots?" Grulle asked, scandalized.

"He lives for it," Dephic said. "It's the best way to tighten discipline when you have a batch of Pretty Polly on the scale of this unit. The Pollution sits up and takes notice, if you follow my meaning. A fresh, dumb replacement can give service exceeding his value if you plink him at the right time, in front of the right audience. We have so many squeakers to teach, I was certain he'd give you a hole in the thinker."

"That's against code," Gole said, his voice weak.

"Yes, that's against code," Dephic shrugged, "but discipline is *in* the code and it's well above all the rest. Your type is expendable. Until you're a few months in the trenches, I don't think you even rightly count as 'living,' no offense."

"None taken." Gole noted, dimly, the call for movement being passed in hand sign. He relayed the command and moved out. Grulle took lead with obvious enthusiasm. He had never been the more useful twin.

They had barely slithered ten minutes when the patrol halted again. Gunshots rang out, then multiplied. A bullet *piffed* into the dirt above Gole's head. A ricochet whined in the distance.

"Contact," Grulle signed unnecessarily. "Pass the word."

"The South!" Gole whispered hoarsely.

Grulle nodded and then jetted away, faster than could possibly be safe, toward the fighting. Gole swam after him through the dirt.

❧ II ❧
THE HAND SQUAD

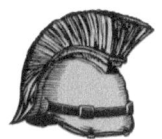

꧁ 5 ꧂

In which Gole Naremsa notices a way to defeat the enemy.

GOLE WAS LAST TO ARRIVE AT THE FIREFIGHT, ANOTHER pinch to his ego. As he crawled up, he discovered he had a good view on the action, with a perspective on both his platoon and the distant ridges of dirt that had their attention. The air was full of gunfire that sounded strangely denuded and innocuous in the slow-moving air.

Rather than rushing in like his Pollution demanded, Gole held back and studied the layout.

The rest of the platoon were muddy shapes, difficult to distinguish from the grime. They had positioned themselves in an arc around the enemy holdout. As far as Gole could see, they had all found good cover. He couldn't see precisely where the platoon was aiming, and he couldn't even tell whether the South was shooting back...*except yes,* by keeping his eyes locked on that far ridge of dirt, he finally picked them out. What looked like a shimmer of hot air was actually fast movement—the southern Tachba popping over the ridge and taking shots. Primitive the Southies might be, but civilization and manners weren't necessary for trench fighting. Their rifles were flawed reproductions of stolen Haphan designs, manufactured in southern factories and unchanged for decades, but they were just as deadly as the robot-tooled Haphan rifles if they found their target.

This group of Southies was outnumbered by Gole's platoon, but it had perfectly synched to the conditions. They were hard to see and they weren't being hit. Even as Gole studied them, they gained the edge in suppressive fire. Soon they had his platoon locked in defensive cover, only able to snap off a few answering rounds at a time.

In a deeper shell hole nearby, Lieutenant Elyseuran lay on his back with a torn fragment of map in his hands. Corphy crawled back and forth the limit of his cover, hectoring the platoon to increase its fire.

None of the boots in the platoon seemed especially concerned. Putting aside the looming possibility of death, the firefight had an almost workaday feel, as if this was long-established and routine procedure, even boring, and they knew how it would play out. Perhaps they expected their greater numbers to tip the scales again. Then, when they locked the southern squad under cover, they would advance and finish them off. That was how it usually worked for Gole at home, during training.

Gole gathered the scene in mere seconds, but the dirt berm in front of his face suddenly danced of its own accord. He realized he was receiving enemy fire. The Southies had picked him out of the dark chaos despite his painted face. He dropped back into cover and moved laterally several yards to another pile of dirt.

Rather than give the enemy another chance by showing himself again, he peeked sideways around his mound of dirt and tried to locate Grulle. The platoon stretched past the enemy position on both sides, halfway encircling it... *In fact,* Gole thought, *one side of the firing line could be sent around the enemy position.* The Southies would not notice a difference in the volume of fire because they already had their enemies suppressed. The platoon could flank them, take them from the side, and destroy them quickly with crossfire.

Gole squirmed to Corphy through the dirt. He said, "The Southies are ripe for flanking and not paying attention."

Corphy barely glanced his way. "So you're an expert now?"

For a moment, Gole fumbled for words.

He was put aback by the strangeness of the sergeant's answer. When it came to fighting and squad-level tactics, *every* Tachba was an expert. Every one of them had trained for this war from five years old, with little variation from household to household. It wasn't as if the eternal front ever changed. Learning about suppression, flanking, and the rest was what made a Tachba childhood tolerable at all.

He tried again. "Three minutes of work and the South is finished."

The sergeant finally focused on him. "Scrag, your only role here is to be fodder. Don't waste my time with fancy dance steps. Your blood-fed is giving high service right next to you. See if you can't do the same."

With that, Corphy crabbed away to yell at someone else.

Gole stared after him.

"Fancy dance steps, neh?" Grulle said by his shoulder. "Golephan, I name ye Dancypants."

"Is he mad?" Gole wondered aloud.

"Dancypants," Grulle nudged his shoulder and broke him out of his thoughts. "Now is time for rifle talk."

Still bewildered, Gole unstrapped his rifle and fed a clip into it.

When the time felt right, he popped out of cover and

emptied the clip. He was safe a moment later, extracting the clip and feeding another. He replayed his movement in his mind—when the Pollution took over, it could make Tachba motions too quick to follow. As far as he could tell, he'd accomplished nothing but spending some rounds. He was only certain he had loosed them toward the enemy, which was the recommended direction.

He emptied two more clips before he rebelled. "This is a waste. I'm going around them."

"We'em break the formy, la?" Grulle asked doubtfully.

"This is a children's firing line, not a formation." Gole pushed backward down the incline, digging his boots into the mumblety dirt to keep from sliding too far. He edged side-ways, searching the dark for a path to the platoon's flank. "Get down here, Grulle. What are you waiting for?"

Grulle slid beside him and slapped a fresh clip into his rifle.

"Stop!" Corphy snapped from behind them.

Gole's muscles locked. "Stopped."

"Stopped-meh," Grulle said.

"Are you squeakers pissing yourselves and running from service, or are you merely acting without orders?"

There's something deeply wrong with this man, Gole thought darkly. It was bad form to give a stop order when it wasn't needed—each use weakened the training and reminded the Tachba how little control they might really have. Stops were only for emergencies, when the Pollution was about to make an impulsive Tachba do something irretrievable. Gole could have used one at the train before he knocked Corphy over. Here, it was overkill. Even worse was asking a question while they were locked down and couldn't answer. It was pure bad manners.

However, Gole had discovered a trick in childhood, to his sister's despair. For the longest time, he had been able to escape Nana's teaching sessions. He envisioned ice-cold water pouring down his spine. He shivered free of the lock and glared at the sergeant.

"Which I'm flanking these Southies myself, sir," he said, "to get this over with. Give me two more boots and I'll get it done faster."

Corphy was so astonished by Gole's immediate response that he didn't have a ready answer.

Of course, Gole had shown Grulle the same trick. Grulle said, "Permission-meh sarnt, get-meh back to-fighting?"

"Get back to it, blood-fed," Corphy said tightly. "Get far away from here if you know what's good for you."

Grulle jabbed a thumb over his shoulder, "La, going-far, sarnt." He scrambled into the dark, precisely the direction Gole had picked, and was quickly out of view. Gole watched him leave with a stab of irritation he knew was unjust. His brother, always so damn eager to please.

He turned back to the sergeant. Corphy was giving him what he supposed was a menacing stare. Really, there were bullets flying! How broken was this man's mind that he couldn't prioritize his attention? Though Gole knew it was the Pollution lashing him to get back to the fight, he let impatience take control of his mouth. "Sergeant, why is the entire platoon hung up on one Southie hand-squad? Why aren't we through them and finishing the patrol already?"

"Lieutenant!" Corphy called over his shoulder. "Pass the word for the lieutenant."

❧ 6 ❧

LIEUTENANT ELYSEURAN SLID NEXT TO THEM A MINUTE later. He looked somehow fresher than the other soldiers, and he took them in with a quick, cheerful grimace. "This one again, sarnt?"

"Which he's not fighting, sir, and now questioning orders."

The humor dropped off the lieutenant's face. "Are you not enjoying the war, Gole?"

"A three minute crawl, sir, and we have South flanked," Gole said quickly. "A crossfire and we either roll them up, or they fall back and we chase them like a hunting party."

"Why do you think we could flank 'em? Fighting from holes is not the same as fighting at home. Three minutes turns into three hours if you get lost."

This is more like it. Whatever Corphy's problem, it didn't afflict the lieutenant. Gole jerked his head back up the route they'd taken. "I saw it as I came in, the whole spread. *I* might get lost, but your regulars? They're lying around shooting into the air. Let's get through these Southies and on with the patrol."

The lieutenant turned to Corphy. "Seems our new general has a fresh idea."

"He's distracting us," Corphy said. "The South is rolled up anyway. Three minutes or thirty minutes, it's over. There's only five of them."

"Three," the lieutenant corrected.

"That couldn't be, sir," Corphy said. "Three fingers in a hand squad?"

"Maybe they're flanking us instead, neh?" The lieutenant joked. He crawled back up and peeked over. "I see two Southies missing every shot, left and right. The one in the middle with the red cap is giving precision fire. That's the thumb of the hand, I'd imagine."

When the lieutenant lowered again, Gole risked a look. One of the Southies, the middle one, indeed wore something on his head. Impossible to tell with this distance and light, but it could have been brown or clay-red.

"The South don't flank," Corphy said shortly. "I think we plinked those first two fingers and the rest of the hand is toiling on."

"Yet the South hasn't been acting like the South lately." The lieutenant thought for a few seconds while the firefight sputtered around them. "Gole, when we get back, I'll talk to you about when to have ideas. Locking down two of us to chat, while under fire? That don't work. Teaching you the rudiments like we're an older sister? That kind of hand-holding is madness out here. Even a blood-fed should see it."

"Yes, sir," Gole said. Honestly, he was surprised the lieutenant had humored him even this far.

"All the same," the lieutenant continued, turning to Corphy, "send some boots around to finish this up. If nothing else, we'll have a new angle on the southern monsters."

"Splitting the unit?" Corphy shook his head. "When we don't need to?"

"Corphor, don't get stubborn on me." Impatience edged the lieutenant's tone.

"Yes, sir. We flank the Southies, and so says the lieuty." Corphy shot Gole a glance of pure malevolence. "I'll send some boots who don't need the world explained to them."

The lieutenant pulled out his map again. "Sergeant, the next time I see you jawing with this squeaker rather than winning the war, I'll question your service. Chatting under fire, really!"

If possible, Corphy filled with more anger. "Which it won't be permitted again."

"Of course it won't. Now send some boots hunting, then get back here and—*ah!*"

Gole and Corphy turned to the lieutenant.

He was a gurgling mess. His jacket was torn open across his belly. He kicked with one leg, stiff with agony, as his stomach spilled into the dirt. His other leg lay at a grotesque angle beneath him. It was connected to his torso only by a seam of canvas and a narrow strap of flesh.

Even as Gole took this in, the lieutenant received another hit. His shoulder slammed into the ground as if it had been stomped by a boot heel. A cloud of blood-moist dirt exploded in their faces.

Gole reeled away from the lieutenant, sliding deeper downwards into cover. Corphy's reflexes were better. He grabbed the lieutenant's belt and pulled him down too.

"From there!" Gole pointed. The shots had come from the side.

From the side!

Corphy dropped the lieutenant and whipped around with his rifle, cutting loose with a full clip where Gole had indicated. He targeted a notch in the ground that Gole hadn't noticed, and sure enough as the rounds impacted the dirt, a shadowy figure emerged and relocated. It was one of the

Southern soldiers, and the Southie had a clear view of the main platoon, which faced the other direction.

"Those hateful scrags," Corphy said, outraged. He swapped clips and cranked off more shots too quickly for Gole to follow. "On the right!" he screamed over his shoulder. "Contact on the right! Move to cover! Enemy contact on the right!"

The platoon responded slowly, as if the order were outside of procedure. The soldiers clambered sideways, trying to reorient. One boot merely rolled on his back to look around —and caught a round in the chin that sent his helmet pinwheeling into the air.

"Fucking shoot your gun!" Corphy screamed in Gole's ear.

Gole snapped awake and fired suppression where he thought the southerner might be. More incoming fire from another direction. Gole reoriented and squeezed off an answer, desperately hunting for the enemy position. *Positions,* because there were two so far. Gole had no idea where to point his stupid rifle.

A Southie hand squad had five fingers, and if three soldiers were in front of them then they had two on their flank. *But what if this is more than just a hand squad?* Gole simply didn't know.

Squad tactics were one thing, but front-line experience was something else entirely. Corphy had Gole beat in that regard, so he checked to see where the sergeant was aiming. Nowhere: Corphy was back at the bottom of the hole, working on the lieutenant. He scooped intestines back into a pile on Elyseuran's stomach and buttoned the coat over it. Then he untwisted the nearly detached leg. All of it seemed pointless and patently unhelpful at the moment.

Gole turned back to the threat. The flanking Southies displaced quickly, shifting positions, snapping off shots on the move. For as long as possible, they would maintain the initiative and prevent the platoon from recovering its balance. There were only two of them, but they quickly knocked down two more of Gole's platoon. Then three. *Then four.*

Corphy was back at Gole's side, bringing his rifle up. He said, "This is getting grim—"

The sergeant's helmet danced, and his head snapped back. He slid down the hole but quickly clambered up again. The Southie bullet had scored a shiny crease into his rilled helmet. His chin strap dangled, broken, and a sheet of blood covered his face where the buckle had sliced his forehead.

"Can't crawl back the way we came," Gole said, "no cover from the crossfire."

"The South was never this smart," Corphy said.

"Orders?" Gole said.

Corphy didn't answer. He tried to see over the lip of the shell hole and received a spray of dirt in his face.

"Orders, sir?" Gole didn't want to browbeat the noncom, but he truly had no idea what should happen next. This situation well and truly exceeded his experience. Surely the calm, professional soldiers he'd seen earlier would know how to handle this.

But Corphy merely shook his head.

"Doggie-gees," said the lieutenant from the bottom of the shell hole. He had to repeat himself, as his voice was too weak to carry over the fire. This was a term that Gole knew at least. The lieutenant meant defensive grenades, the ones shaped like cans rather then the round ones used on the offense.

"Right, and doggie-gees it is," Corphy said, relief clear.

Gole had just grabbed a grenade out of his satchel when a whistle sounded. The sharp sound pierced the high crackle of rifle fire, and it came from the direction of the flanking Southies. It wasn't them whistling, however. It came from *behind* them and it was a northern signal: two rising shrieks that meant "watch fire."

The platoon's fire dropped away, and a volley of shots emitted near the Southerner's positions. A quick exchange of fire.

Another.

Then silence.

A face appeared over a ledge of dirt, right in Gole's gunsight.

"Grulle!" he shouted.

The blood-fed grinned and made a crude gesture at Gole.

The three original Southies, still in their strong position, unleashed a volley at Grulle with every sign of displeasure. He dropped quickly back into cover.

It was clear to everyone what had just happened. The blood-fed had circled behind the flankers and taken them out. The flankers had themselves been flanked.

The platoon was free to turn its attention back to the remaining Southies.

"All right you scrags," Corphy yelled, "clear out that nest."

They moved with something Gole hadn't seen yet: real anger. It was as if the flanking trick had made it personal. The platoon charged overland, firing whenever possible, but aggressively closing the distance to the enemy's position. Gole followed on their heels, causing no discernible damage with his own shots.

When the platoon was close enough, they filled the Southie's position with oggie-gees. The offensive grenades went off with a string of pops, louder than the gunfire.

When they finally crested the Southie's position, they found the pit empty. The enemy had already fled.

7

THE RETURN TO THE TRENCH WAS NOT THE RELIEF GOLE expected. The Pollution picked that moment, finally, to make him feel invincible. He crept behind his tireless blood-fed, hating the world, even hating the soldiers around him, and nearly vibrating with the desire to turn around and single-handedly attack the South. Someone in a red cap deserved punishment—for tricking the patrol, for treating them all like children, for shooting the only officer who actually seemed reasonable and sane.

"Heard you got the lieutenant killed," said a voice underneath Gole.

It was the soldier from earlier, the one who liked sarcasm. Dephic. The platoon had paused for a minute's rest, and they were all so covered in filth that Gole had crawled across him like another mound of dirt.

"The lieutenant isn't dead," Gole said, shifting to the side. "And it wasn't me, it was the South."

"You didn't salute him, none? I swear I told someone not to salute at the front." Dephic followed as Gole tried to get away. "Not sure if it was you or some other squeaker."

Gole muttered, "I only pointed out we could hit the Southies from the side. The lieutenant had just decided to try it, and he pulled out his map. That's when they hit *us* from the side."

"Nah, Southies don't hit from the side."

Gole almost faltered, perplexed. "Were we at the same gunfight?"

"Dephic means that the front is full of confusing shit," said a new voice. Yet another soldier rolled over in the mud, directly in Gole's path. This one was the old-timer, Malley. "The South don't crawl a hundred yards to shoot you from the side, not when you're ten yards in front of them."

"I feel I have to insist," Gole said evenly, though he felt like he was going mad. "Someone killed six of the platoon, and shot the lieutenant's leg off."

"Oh, that was the South, all right," Dephic said. "But it was some other accident, and we only caught the fall-out. Maybe it was part of a different hand-squad."

"Maybe it was the same hand-squad," Malley suggested, "but the two flankers were coming back from fetching something and they got lucky."

"Or maybe they were always there, and we simply put ourselves in a bad spot," Dephic said. "Don't make the South out to be anything but witless primitives. Don't give them credit for something that was probably a simple accident. The eternal front loves a good joke."

"You said the lieutenant pulled his map out," Malley added. "That made him a prime target. Officers are the first to get plinked, so they need to hide who they are."

A boot further up turned to them. "Which there's a lot of chatter here, and we haven't re-assed the trench yet."

Dephic only laughed. "Hlallady, you think the monsters are following us, la?"

"Like they suddenly turned clever?" Malley added scornfully. But the certainty was gone from his voice, and they fell quiet.

As for Gole, as soon as the idea was proposed, he felt crosshairs on his back. He wormed through the dirt, witnessing himself from behind through Red Cap's eyes, and his spine burned with anticipation. He knew the exact spot the bullet would hit...

The trench opened under his hands and he fell over the parapet. He didn't even try to catch himself. He landed on his side and folded open. Staring at a sky that seemed almost as dirty and corrupted as the trench itself, he tried to feel safe with the walls around him.

A drumbeat resonated through the earth. A soft wallop, followed by more. An artillery barrage starting up. Strange that he felt it in the ground before hearing it in the air.

"What happens next?" Gole asked when Malley dropped into the trench. Dephic and Grulle entered next. All of them landed more gracefully than Gole.

"You mean for us? The platoon?" Malley scratched his chin. "Probably the South has an answer for the fingers we chopped off. We'll repulse a small probe. A friendly exchange."

"Sounds relaxing."

Dephic turned alertly. "That was more sarcasm, wasn't it?"

"Yes, it was," Malley said. "Gole is a sarcastic little scrag."

"Lovely, just lovely."

Grulle caught Gole's eyes and grinned. It was as if the blood-fed knew what Gole was thinking, and maybe he did. Blood-fed twins weren't more stupid than their brothers, not really; it was nothing so simple. They merely lacked the persistence for continuous engagement with the world. Until the day a blood-fed bolted into true maturity, they lived small beads of life, each bead only tenuously connected to the last.

"That's what is next for you." Gole said. "What's next for *me?*"

"Oh, you caught that?" Dephic shrugged. "They said you was too clever, no offense."

Malley patted Gole's shoulder in an almost fatherly manner. "No doubt, you'll be executed for disobeying orders, ye dumb scrag."

Gole bolted upright. "What? I obeyed my orders."

"There was lots of talk and not much shooting. I think that'll be the topic."

"I shot at the dirt, the same as the rest of you."

"Probably a firing squad," Dephic mused. He fixed Gole with a sudden intense look and said, "*You will be executed and then fall to the ground.* Was that sarcastic?"

"No, Dephic," Malley said. "Sarcasm would be more like, *We will miss your contributions to the 51st.*"

"But we won't?"

"Not in the slightest."

Gole swiveled between them. He hoped this was some of that famous trench humor. Cruel jokes for brutal soldiers fighting a savage war. It had to be that.

8

Corphy dropped into their midst from above. He landed lightly and snapped orders as more boots lowered the lieutenant into the trench. Elyseuran was white as new snow. They had tied his wounded leg to his sound leg, which was strange. Gole would have expected it to be left behind. The devastation of the lieutenant's shoulder made that quarter of his torso gruesomely pliant. There was simply not enough bone structure left for the body to keep its shape in the coat. The arm would be a loss too. As for the lieutenant's ruined stomach, it was now packed with the sergeant's coat and held closed with two more belts. Thanks to the ancient twisting, the Tachba could recover quickly from the most terrible wounds. Even so, the lieutenant looked like a hopeless case.

Corphy noticed Gole's attention. "See what happens when a squeaker is permitted to create a distraction?"

Gole opened his mouth to answer, but Corphy didn't let him. With a full-bodied punch to the sternum, he sent Gole flying across the trench. As Gole landed on the ground, Grulle loomed behind the sergeant.

"Stop," Corphy snapped, not turning.

Grulle's trench knife hesitated against the base of Corphy's skull.

"Grulle, don't," Gole said, wheezing for breath.

They waited while Grulle negotiated the issue with Pretty Polly. She would be confusing the blood-fed with two urges at once. The first, to protect his milk-fed brother and his valuable decision-making skills. The second, to obey authority.

The outcome wasn't in question. Grulle shared the basic, amiable disposition of most blood-fed, and he always shied from confrontation. His stop-training was also faultless. Grulle sheathed his knife and stepped back.

"Scrag," Corphy continued, staring at Gole, "when I talked about distraction I wasn't talking to you, I was talking to the others. *You* are past talking to. You are now the object lesson for all the other squeakers we've sucked into our ranks in the last few weeks. Much more of this and we'll be half green, and I'm weary in my bones of explaining right discipline."

Corphy turned to the rest of the men in the trench. "Even worse, boots, is having to explain orders while *under fire.* That's barbaric. We are soldiers of the Haphan Empire. We don't question our officers, we follow orders or the very Empire falls. We follow orders, or *this* happens."

He nudged Elyseuran's leg with his boot.

The lieutenant winced and stirred. "So sarnt finally gets to make a new speech." He managed to smile, though it was gruesome, his mouth lined with blood. "Boys, I don't expect I'll be back."

"Give you joy, sir," Dephic said.

"Eh? For what?" The lieutenant cracked an eye and frowned at him.

"Which you'll finally meet the ancestors face to face," Dephic explained. "We'll speak to you through the fire."

"Hold on, man," the lieutenant shot back. "I don't plan on

dying! Don't throw my corpse out of the trench just yet. Sergeant, don't let Dephic be the one to check whether I'm dead."

The boots laughed. Even Corphy unclenched slightly.

"And no, that wasn't sarcasm, Dephic," the lieutenant added, to more laughter. Then he shuddered with pain and drew serious. "I'll give you a little dead-talking, though. Maybe...maybe listen like this is the last thing I'll ever say. Keep your eyes open out there, boys. Something strange is happening in the South. Something odd is changing our special little war."

"What odd, sir?" Malley's tone was uneasy.

"If I knew, I'd dead-talk it at you, wouldn't I, you blood-fed scrag?" The lieutenant softened it with a tight grin. "All I know is that it's changing. The great snake of the front is shifting in its dreams. I am...I am Lieutenant Panthan Elyseuran. I am proud to have done service with all of you."

"Service," the men murmured.

Corphy nodded at the two boots who had lowered the lieutenant into the trench. "You'll bring him back to the staging area."

"La, to hospital?" one asked doubtfully.

"Hospital! Do you hate your lieutenant? No, we're taking him directly to unit HQ. The lieutenant has always been too friendly by half, even with the Happies. Maybe he'll reap some goodwill and get their good medicine." Corphy shifted to Gole. "You're coming with us. To ensure your obedience, your blood-fed will remain here with the unit. Make this clear to your idiot."

Gole clenched his jaw, turning to his brother. Grulle understood perfectly and looked stricken.

Not enough time to think! This had gone off the rails so quickly. It was like when their brother had thought he could jump off the roof and land safely on a bed of rocks; Gole felt incredulity, anger, and sorrow all stirred together. It would be Corphy's report against his, *and* escalated to the overlords' attention. Nothing good could possibly come of it.

Indeed, there was a fair chance Gole would never return. He had no avenue he could see, no choice but to finally catch Grulle's eyes. He said, "Stay here, my Best Little Bird."

Grulle wavered until Malley crossed to him and took his hand. The kindness in the gesture nearly broke Gole with shame.

CORPHY LED THE WAY THROUGH THE TRENCHES. THE TWO boots carried the unconscious lieutenant by his good shoulder and his good leg. Gole followed behind.

Pollution, come distract me, Gole thought. He cinched the strap of his rifle over his jacket so its tightness could damp the tightness in his chest. *Pretty Polly, bump me with your hip.*

In a few minutes, Gole knew, his brother's worry would unwrinkle. Gole wouldn't disappear from his blood-fed's mind; he would only be separate. Gole would exist in a different bubble from the present world—and if Grulle never saw Gole again, that bubble would never change. Gole would always be recent, always be on the verge of return.

In a few minutes, too, the Pollution would separate Gole from his own concerns. He should relish his worry while it was still raw and austere, but he couldn't. Real sorrow felt vile. He would miss the honest feeling when it was gone—but he wouldn't wish it back.

Because just imagine if his Pollution broke and every bleak feeling returned in a flood! Gole had grown up with five, then four, then *two* pairs of brothers. To him, they were all distinct faces and personalities. They were smiles and laughter and clever plans. They had all turned silent and transparent, converting to memory and mood, as their Pollution brought them to one ruin or another.

If Gole was walking toward punishment...well, the punishment for misbehavior under fire was a summary execution. He didn't disagree with it in concept. It was important to prune the over-polluted scrags before their aberrations triggered worse in other soldiers. If this was really happening, however, Gole was *sad*. He was supposed to have accomplished a little more with his life. He'd hoped for a little more than this.

The change occurred.

At its strongest, the Pollution was always Pretty Polly. She kissed his ear. She brushed her lips over his forehead and smiled. Her gaze was full of understanding. And as always, there were other shapes behind her, just out of focus. The ancient encoded memories, the ones that were the same for all Tachba men. The thoughts that couldn't be explained with words.

Gole's concern lifted off his shoulders and sloughed into the air. Nauseating at first, then a relief. He let determination fill him. He felt a brisk confidence that he'd win through this next challenge. Anything that came up, he'd spot a way through it.

He didn't think about the falseness that cloaked the servitor controls. He leaned into them, letting them catch on the corners of his mind. In moments, the thoughts were indistinguishable from his own.

Grulle would be okay.

Corphy would see reason.

Dephic would learn sarcasm.

Gole would have a chance to kill that Southie in the red cap.

9

THEIR DESTINATION PUT THE PLATOON'S FORWARD TRENCH to shame. The reserve trench was more like a city thorough-fare, with space for soldiers moving both directions and more to stand watch over the parapet. Even wheelbarrows of food and ammunition could pass side-by-side on the wide plank flooring. The sandbags looked stiff, new, and didn't rain dust when Gole brushed against them. Corphy turned at last into an alcove that could nearly be called a patio.

The walls were twelve feet tall, high enough to cast shade on the Haphan officers of the 51st Ville Emsa Fusiliers. Under a tight awning, tables and chairs filled the small space. Timber-braced doorways in every wall showed stairways leading to deep bunkers.

The Haphans were gathered over a map on the table. Their clean gray uniforms made Gole conscious of his own grimy trench kit. Funny how that worked, as Gole had been self-conscious of its newness just hours earlier.

One of the officers glanced up, then straightened.

"Ah, Sergeant Caremsa?" The Haphan spoke in perfect, clipped Tachbavim. He came around the table, ignoring their salutes. Where the other Haphans seemed pinched and closed, this one's face was more open and seemed to invite their gaze. Though his coat was buttoned to his throat even in the pervasive heat, he was the least fussy of the cluster, with scruffy cheeks and sweat-slicked hair. Gole studied his sash and deciphered that this was a colonel, possibly a lieutenant colonel. That would put him above the company's Tachba low colonel.

The Haphan noticed the body on the ground. "Oh dear, is that…"

"Which it's the lieutenant," Corphy said. "Got a thump while on patrol. Didn't need to, either. Could have been avoided."

"Panthan," the colonel said. His tone was precisely that of a disappointed father. "Regrettable. He had such high function. So much promise."

"Which I failed to mention he's not dead, sir," Corphy added.

"Of course he isn't." The colonel looked doubtful. "That leg."

"Still attached, sir. He still has most of his intestine."

"Then maybe there's hope. Maybe he'll be serviceable again." The colonel glanced at a Tachba aide hovering in the corner. "Wick, grab some helpies and carry the lieutenant to the Haphan forward hospital. Tag him for the good medicine. Ah, on my family account, I suppose."

He turned back to Corphy, looking slightly miffed. "Panthan Elyseuran is too good to waste," he said, as if to convince himself.

"The men asked how long he might be on the mend, sir."

"For what I see? A year at least. Maybe he'll take some training, keep his brain engaged. Officer school. If he doesn't go mad, he'll lead a company himself when he gets back."

"Emperor's service!" Corphy exclaimed.

"Yes, sergeant. Tell that to his men. Lieutenant Panthan Elyseuran will be made whole and raised to higher leadership. I will send the order myself, *written down,* in not five minute's time."

One of the boots who had carried the lieutenant exclaimed, "Written!" Then, "Begging your pardon, very, sir."

"Given." The colonel waved a hand. "A good officer has good men, they say. Of course you're overwhelmed. You're overflowing with gratitude for me."

"Yes, sir," Corphy said.

The Haphan went still with thought. Gole admired how he did that. The other Haphans at the table were nearly motionless as well, only one of them drumming his fingers on the map as they whispered back and forth. Compared to the Haphans, the Tachba were twitchy bundles, never still: always a leg bouncing, a head rocking, a clenched and shaking hand that had to be hidden even when no one looked.

"I suppose you'll need promotion, Corphy," the colonel finally said. Corphy twitched with tension.

"Yes, there's no helping it," the colonel continued. "Corphor Caremsa: for your service to the Empire, I commission you into the Sesseran chivalry. You are promoted, sir, to half lieutenant."

Corphy nodded convulsively. The two soldiers behind him murmured, "Give you joy, sir."

"That's a bump to *half* lieutenant, you hear?" The colonel tilted closer. "You'll have the platoon for now but it's not confirmed. We've been losing officers left and right, so you might get shuffled later."

"Yes, sir."

"We don't even have a Tacchie captain for the company right now! Your Colonel Goldros wants to fill the spots, but I'm tired of waiting. I'll personally inform him about your promotion. Let him bitch at me directly if he doesn't like it.

I'm sure I'll get an earful. If there's ever a Tacchie who makes me nervous!" The colonel laughed, alone.

"Thank you sir," Corphy said. "Not a bump I expected, sir."

"Nonsense, you're a, uh, feasible investment. Don't let it ever be said that I'm generous. At least, don't let it be said outside of my hearing." The colonel paused again, but Corphy only nodded. "Well, that's handled, then."

Corphy glanced up. "Which—"

"I know, Corphor. This creature with the hangdog face." The Haphan's gray eyes flickered to Gole, then returned to Corphy. "What's he done?"

"Sir, which he argued over orders! On patrol, between the trenches, in the middle of a fire-fight. Which he drew the lieutenant into the argument, and caused the lieutenant to be killed! Nearly."

Gole flushed with anger, but the Haphan didn't seem to notice.

"He's one of our raw recruits, then, lieutenant? A new scrag who doesn't know anything?"

"Yes, sir. I'm happy to agree with you, he is as dumb as a corpse," Corphy said. Then he added, "Which he also violated a corpse!"

The Haphans at the table coughed all at once.

"Ye gods. When did this lascivious creature arrive on the front?"

"This morning, sir."

"He has been busy, hasn't he?" The colonel finally shifted to Gole. His face was exquisitely unreadable.

"Yes, sir!" Corphy said. "This morning, when I were pushing the scrags into line, he kissed me one! Er, he struck me, sir."

Gole had been struggling to hold himself still and had managed to be as still as the Haphan, even through the mention of Yaelaphan's corpse. At this last, however, he said, *"That?"*

Corphy turned to him. Whatever deferential terror he felt when facing the Haphan colonel melted away when he faced Gole. "'That' what, scrag?"

"That, *sir?*"

The table coughed again, even louder.

"Soldier," the colonel said, addressing Gole. "Were you not advised against striking your superiors? I'm sure it's in a manual somewhere."

To Gole, that sounded like permission to finally speak. "Yes sir. It's in Section 3, Verse 10 of the Sesseran Military Code. I would never knowingly strike a superior, and I didn't think I was striking one at the time."

The colonel's eyebrow arched. "So? You sometimes simply throw a punch and hope for the best? I've heard worse, actually."

"It was about my blood-fed, sir," Gole said. "As we marshaled for review, my brother Grulle was punched in the neck *from behind* and he fell at my feet. I simply knocked over the scrag who hit him."

Corphy twitched like he was itching to hit someone again.

Well, Gole thought, *it's not like I can get into more trouble.* He gave his tongue free license. "So you see, Colonel, nobody would have thought they were striking a superior. They would have thought they were only striking a coward who punches people from behind as they enter the trenches to serve the empire."

The colonel's eyes shifted between Gole and the new lieutenant. Corphy shook visibly. Gole's blood hummed, too, with freshly recollected outrage. The Pollution wanted some salutary violence to result from this discussion. He kept himself as still as possible, repressing every tremor.

"I think the story begins to take shape," the colonel said.

"If it please the colonel—" Corphy started.

"Lieutenant Caremsa," the colonel said, then softened his tone. "Corphor, do you believe your leadership and your example can rehabilitate this soldier? Remember, I need every squeaker I have. A boot with a blood-fed he cares about is worth three singletons."

Had the Haphan phrased it as an order, it would have been easier for Corphy to answer. As it was, the man had to think. He shivered, then said, "Of course, sir. I believe I can do something with this creature."

"I have the highest confidence in you, lieutenant." The colonel's eyes were still on Gole. "I will heed your wise advice, then. There will be no summary execution for this new boot. Let's see how he develops, shall we?"

"Thank you, sir," Corphy grated.

"You, boy." The colonel stepped close, and looked up into Gole's face. "How old are you?"

"Fourteen, sir," Gole answered. "And a half."

"Name?"

"Golephan Naremsa, of the House Naremsa."

"*House* Naremsa, eh? An old house?"

"Since before paper and thought," said Gole automatically.

"*Since what?*" The colonel's voice turned sharp.

"Since before paper and thought," Gole repeated, and finally realized his error.

'Before paper and thought' meant Gole's family had been established before the Haphans conquered the province. Since before the Empire had colonized the planet, in fact. The Naremsa family had already been occupying its land when the Haphans issued the deed of ownership. The Overlords did not like their servitors to be aware of pre-landing history.

The colonel's face nearly communicated something, and

Gole stared at it, fascinated. He'd heard that Haphans lived far longer than the Tachba's average forty years, sometimes past eighty or beyond. He had thought their impassivity might be the result of such terrible longevity. This Haphan was only middle-aged, however, in his early twenties but already inscrutable. It was something he'd learned—and something Gole could learn.

The colonel's voice turned fractionally sharp. "Since before the empire invested this world, you mean. Since before we civilized your barbaric people, including this little kingdom of Sessera."

"Perhaps," Gole said, and inwardly cursed himself.

"Perhaps?" the colonel repeated.

"Yes, sir. You see, that was all before my time."

The Haphan's face didn't change, nothing so vulgar. Yet Gole thought he saw amusement flicker in the Haphan's eyes.

"Nicely put, Golephan Naremsa of the House Naremsa," the colonel said. "I am Lord Count Seul Tan Luscetian, Lieutenant Colonel in the Haphan Imperial Expeditionary Land Forces. Acquaintance."

Even Gole knew this one. He tipped forward from the hip. "Acquaintance."

"Keep this one alive for me, lieutenant," the colonel said, finally turning away. "I have every confidence, every confidence. Now I must see about getting some new scouts to your part of the line."

10

THOUGH HE WAS NOW THE MOST WELL-TRAVELED replacement in the 51st, Gole still hadn't learned the trench layout. When they brought the wounded lieutenant to Colonel Luscetian, Gole had been wrapped in his dire thoughts and staring at the ground. Now, returning to his platoon in the 51st, he struggled to keep up with Corphy.

The new-made lieutenant walked at a boil, snapping at anyone who strayed into his path. He never checked whether Gole was following, probably hoping Gole would go missing.

Since Corphy and the two soldiers kept disappearing around traverses ahead of him, Gole found his home trench nearly unassisted and navigating by instinct. He came upon it with surprise and relief. Grulle glanced up and nodded, as if he had merely returned from the latrine.

Malley sat with Grulle, and seemed to be asleep until he cracked an eye. "You missed dinner."

"Of course I did." Gole sagged against the sandbags and let gravity pull him to the ground. So long as there were no further surprises, this would be his first chance to rest since they'd embarked the trench train this morning. "Malley, how come I'm not dead?"

The old-timer shrugged. "I don't know. Give it time?"

"I thought I was walking to my summary, and yet here I am."

"Are you saying you didn't get your summary?"

Again, Gole had the feeling of missing something crucial. When would these people start making sense? "We're talking about summary *execution*, aren't we?"

"Of course." Malley thought a moment. "I understand. You're wondering why, if you've been executed, you're still walking around."

Grulle went tense. "Ghost?"

"No, boy, not a ghost." Malley leaned forward. "Now Gole, here's the book on summary executions. The Happies don't shoot their Tachba at the front because it would destroy the unit's morale. Can you imagine if we were being shot at from both South *and* North? No. First you 'get' your summary, and when the unit is relieved, you're 'given' your summary. That's when you're put against the wall. They laser you to pieces— and when it comes to your health, I've heard it's conclusive. We're due some rest leave soon."

"In three or four days," said the pile of sandbags Gole was sitting on.

Gole jumped, then moved to the side. Dephic again, nestled in the pile. "Dephic, how are you always underfoot?"

"Why do you never look where you sit?" Dephic shrugged. "Anyway, we go four weeks on, four days off, and we've now been front-lined for three-and-a-half weeks. Normally I can't count the days, but I remember something the lieutenant said. He said the Fusiliers are fifteen percent understrength thanks to attrition. Fifteen percent! That *has* to be more than half of the unit, neh? The lieutenant said the percentage was, uh, *untoward and unwonted*. He were talking about how many of our asses have been plinked on our so-called quiet mile of front."

Malley nodded. "Which that's a high number, to be sure. But the lieutenant should not have mentioned the dead until we went on rest leave. Talking about our lost boots, it gets the eternal front thinking about you. What if it thinks you're criticizing the war? The front won't tolerate spiteful talk, it will sooner strike you down. I'd remind the lieutenant myself, except he's poorly."

"I didn't receive a summary," Gole finally blurted.

They were surprised. Even Grulle stared, if only because the others were already staring.

Gole continued, "The Haphan bumped Corphy to half lieutenant—"

"Not full lieutenant, eh? That will sting the little tyrant."

"—And the Haphan colonel told him to rehabilitate me."

"That sounds like a Haphan colonel, all right," Dephic said. "They're trying to conserve us, since we're being spent so quickly."

"What's our Haphan like?" Malley asked.

Now Gole was surprised. "You haven't met him?"

"No-meh, scrag," Malley snickered at the idea. "But then, I didn't kill a lieutenant my first day in the trench."

"For the last time, it wasn't me that killed the lieutenant. And he's not dead, anyway."

"Ye jus' winged him, neh?" Grulle shot him a wicked grin.

Gole said, "The lieutenant was sent to the Haphan hospital for the 'good' medicine. He'll be patched up, they said, and sent to officer school."

Malley and Dephic sighed with relief.

"Gole," Grulle said softly, "I kept you a pocket of dinner."

"Food?" Gole brought himself back. "Where is it?"

"Which I forgot, and ate it out of the same pocket."

Gole laughed. "Thank you for the thought, brother."

"You feel-better now, la?"

"Never better," Gole said. "First, I wasn't summarily executed. Now, a brief thought of food."

"More sarcasm again, just lovely," Dephic sighed. "That's classic Gole."

Malley shoved a heel of bread and a round stone into Gole's hand. The stone turned out to be hard cheese, the kind that would soften in the mouth if it could be hammered into smaller pieces.

They fell into amiable silence to watch Gole eat. This was another manifestation of the Pollution, Gole knew, in all its unpredictable facets. *We'll share out even the smallest pleasures.*

In the silence, they heard a watery sob.

It came from above them, by the lip of the trench.

Malley shook his head before Gole could be alarmed. "Which it's just Yaelaphan, feeling gassy."

Another gasp.

"Temperature changing, getting toward night," Malley added. "Gives them indigestion in the gut."

Gole took another bite of bread but had to stop again at a loud eruption of flatulence. Then, out the other side, a soft, wheezing moan.

"Which Yaellie could never shut up," Malley said, in pure annoyance. He shouted to the top of the trench, "Which I thought we'd get some peace when you was plinked, ye scrag!"

"Shh, Malley." Dephic snuggled deeper in his pile of empty sandbags. "He's a good fellow. It's nice to hear him again."

Further from the trench, deeper in the dark, another bubbling gasp. Then, from even further away, another voice expelled a warbling sigh, saying something nearly intelligible. Sound at the edge of meaning.

They listened as the field of bodies outside the trench awoke.

"A proper friendly chat," Dephic murmured.

"Words in the dark, la," Grulle said.

❧ III ❦

NIGHT PATROL

11

In which Gole Naremsa attempts to save his comrades.

GOLE, GRULLE, MALLEY, DEPHIC, AND A SOLDIER THEY'D met earlier, Hlallady, sheltered through the night. They slept in a knot of interleaved limbs, linked arms, and heads resting on gurgling stomachs. Once, Gole bolted from a dream where he was kicking through frictionless dirt, chased by an unknown terror. He found himself mired in the human raft. Snores in his ear, a boot heel in his crotch. He fell back to sleep, relieved.

Gole didn't rouse the next morning, and nobody came to rouse him through the day. The sun was dipping again when the sound of activity brought him fully awake: a group of soldiers filtering into the trench to sit with them. Though they arrived at different times and hardly spoke, they seemed connected to each other. It wasn't their trench kit or their faces but something in their methodical and watchful manner. These men weren't as twitchy as the regular line soldiers. Gole's guess was confirmed when a hard-faced Low Sergeant with a permanent frown squatted beside him.

"Golephan Naremsa," he said.

"What do you want, sarnt?" Dephic snapped, with a coldness that was unlike him. Gole sat up.

The sergeant ignored Dephic. "Me'em Nadros Nophalemsa, your sergeant. You and your blood-fed are with me now."

"But Gole's a squeaker!" Dephic said.

"So is Grulle," Gole said, annoyed. "Anyway, sarnt, I will give service."

"That's not what I heard." Nadros looked him up and down. "Re-gear yourself and your blood-fed. No kit, no lug, and going over easy."

"Yes, sir," Gole said.

Behind Nadros, Malley shook his head.

The sergeant swung away, then turned back. "Listen, scrag, there's no room for the Pollution on night patrol. No room for talk. Use your hand sign. If you can't see a hand, you will do nothing. If we forget you, you will wait in the mud until the South finds you and kills you. Then when you're dead, be a quiet corpse. If your corpse makes a sound before daylight, la, I'll cut you open and shit in your stomach."

"Someone *finally* shitting in Gole's stomach?" Grulle asked.

Nadros jerked a thumb at the blood-fed. "Can you control this creature?"

"Yes, sir," Gole signed.

"Don't make me kill you," the sergeant finished. He climbed out of his crouch and returned to his men, who still hadn't said a word. They were shedding equipment in the trench.

Gole turned back to the others. "What's going on?"

Malley shook his head again. "You're a night fighter now, looks like. You do night patrols. Many chances for service."

"I don't understand," Gole said. "Didn't we patrol last night? What was that?"

"That was a *patrol at night*," Dephic said. "Sergeant Nadros does *night patrol*. The first kind is a simple sweep. The second kind is where you're looking for trouble. Actively hunting for monsters. Get the difference?"

"Many chances for service," Malley said again, looking away.

Gole didn't need any further explanation. The stock phrase among boots was: "Many chances for service, which must be passed up, it wouldn't serve." As bluntly as the Pollution would allow a subversive idea, he was being told to be careful with himself. On night patrol, apparently, there would be many chances to make a misstep and never return.

He glanced at Grulle, who was already dropping his extra gear. His twin fumbled over the clasp to his ammunition sack but got it to work. Gole caught the sack and fastened it again over his brother's shoulder.

"You keep this one," he murmured. "It has rifle food."

Grulle grinned. "Whoops! Like sister taught-meh."

"Nana loves you," Gole added. He paused, surprised at himself.

"Me'em love the crazy little witch," Grulle replied. He glanced around. "La, where is she?"

"Home," Gole said. "Do you remember home?"

Grulle snorted at him.

"I guess Nana is teaching the next crop of boys now. Do you remember your little brothers?"

Grulle went thoughtful, by which Gole knew his blood-fed was now returning them to his mind. Gole didn't want his brother to lose them, ever. "Do you remember growing up, Grulendon?"

"Ye scrag." Grulle ruffled his hair fondly. "What for, remember-meh the days? I have you, little rock."

Hlallady had seemed to be asleep, but now he kicked Gole's boot, hard. "Damn your sister and damn your home, squeakers. No talk of that out here."

"Listen to Hlallie," Dephic said, shifting his eyes off the twins. "Pretty Polly don't pick you up after thinking about home."

Gole turned and unbuckled his own satchel, which he'd worn through the night without noticing as he slept like death. The others were right. The Pollution wouldn't sweep away homesickness with all the other unproductive sentiments. How properly appalling that Gole could be more cheerful walking to a summary execution than remembering his childhood.

SERGEANT NADROS'S SQUAD MUSTERED WHEN THE SKY turned dark.

"What, no ladder?" Gole asked, and regretted it when the other boots snickered. Their faces were blacked, and their kit was grimy canvas with not a metal button or latch to reflect the moonlight. Indeed, they were almost invisible already, just a few feet away. When they entered the airy darkness, they would disappear completely.

"No ladder, scrag," said one of the men. "We levitate this-wise, like spirits." He launched off the step-up and caught the parapet of the trench under his arm. For a moment he simply hung off the edge, staring into the dark.

"Helmet," Nadros whispered.

The man passed his helmet back down. The rest of the squad placed theirs on the packs where they wouldn't roll into each other. Though he'd only donned his helmet a moment earlier, Gole felt lightheaded and exposed when he took it off again.

"Naught seen," came the whisper from above.

The rest of the squad soundlessly flung themselves up the trench wall, catching the parapet with elbows or knees. Gole could jump like that—all Tachba could—but only if he didn't think about it too long first.

Grulle leapt for the wall. The sergeant snatched him out of the air and put him back on the ground. "You practice that later, blood-fed, hear me?"

"Hear," Grulle said.

Nadros cradled his hands and gave Grulle, and then Gole, a boost to the edge. They made it silently over the top and into the landscape.

Perhaps the sergeant had heard about Gole and Yaelaphan because they were a good ten yards away from the expressive corpse. Nadros tapped his shoulder, and he in turn tapped Grulle's.

"Do I need to say it? Silence discipline."

They nodded.

"You will follow the..." The sergeant trailed off, perplexed. The boots ahead of them were still nearby in the darkness. They had not moved forward.

"What, la?" Nadros hissed. He glanced at Gole. "The silence discipline is just for you two."

The word was passed, man to man, back to the sergeant. "Which there's fresh tape laid out. But it goes a different direction."

The sergeant ruminated over this, which puzzled Gole. They were literally three feet from their home trench. What was there to think about already? And why were they so fixated on using tape?

"Where's the old tape?" Nadros asked.

The word traveled forward, then back. "Which it's gone from the ground."

Nadros fixed Gole with a glance. "Did you have a batch of scouts in the trench today?"

"Slept through day," Grulle signed.

"Figures."

Gole leaned close and whispered, "But the Haphan colonel mentioned getting scouts to our part of the trench."

"You saw him yesterday, after you killed the lieutenant?"

Gole nodded, unwillingly.

"Did he mention the scouts in your hearing? I mean, in Corphy's hearing?"

Gole nodded again.

Nadros frowned. "Then he wanted us to hear and to know."

"Why-dithering?" Grulle whispered.

Nadros said, "Pass the word, we follow the tape."

❧ 12 ❧

AFTER A MERE THIRTY MINUTES OF BELLYING OVER SOFT soil, the patrol stopped. Nadros, who had been keeping station behind the brothers and watching them with baleful eyes, now squirmed forward.

"What?" he signed.

"Contact." Hand sign was derived from hunting signals, and the word the boot used was "spore of scavenger."

"Thrills!" Grulle signed with a wide smile.

The sergeant moved forward to assess the situation, finally leaving them alone. Gole turned to another soldier in the dark and signed, "Is it always this quick?"

The soldier shook his head. Behind the blacking, he seemed uneasy. He signed, "Sparse prey this close to camp."

A quiet aeon where Gole nestled between the two others. Grulle breathed on his neck from one side, the anonymous soldier breathed from the other.

Finally the boots ahead shifted.

"Creep till sighting," came the signal.

They slithered toward a low rise in the earth. Earlier in the day, Malley had mentioned that this sector of the trench had been static for easily sixty years. This explained the preternatural softness of the ground—the regular landscape had long ago been pulverized into fine dust. The endless artillery barrages shifted the earth like dunes in a desert, building temporary hillocks and then blasting them down and shifting them elsewhere.

As Gole crawled up the slope, which was no higher than a crouching man, he pictured how the earth beneath them had been sterilized by innumerable exploding shells. The soil would be as clean as a knife blade in a fire, even despite the constant rain of blood and bodies at the top. No root systems, no strata in the soil, very few clods. The earth was fine and unstructured, still undifferentiated even thirty feet down. They knew this from the sappers, Malley explained, because they complained how deep they had to dig to make tunnels and bunkers that wouldn't quickly collapse.

The sergeant gestured Gole closer, and Grulle followed.

"Head down," Nadros signed. "Stay away from edge. Don't startle them. Do like this."

They watched how Nadros did it. The sergeant raised his chest off the ground and looked over the crest of dirt without disturbing it. In the air, the sergeant seemed to pulse—the Pollution kicking in, matching his stealthy movement to the faint breeze that blew from the South and caused airborne dust to roil over itself. It was a minor effect but it could add full seconds before an enemy might pick them out of the night.

The sergeant eased back down, brow knitted. Then he glanced at Gole and gestured for him to look.

Gole mimicked Nadros's actions. He wasn't sure if he, too, shifted in the breeze. That part worked best when it wasn't thought about. Instead, he focused on what could be seen over the crest of dirt.

Near the bottom of the hole, less than eight yards distant,

a small candle was stuck in the earth. It illuminated three shadowy figures. Two were waiting by a darker blot in the ground, and a third was dragging a munitions box toward them. The box was heavy, based on the depth of the track it left in the dirt. Gole stayed just long enough for his eyes to focus, and then lowered himself back down.

Nadros gestured again, and Grulle took his turn.

The sergeant leaned close. "So, you saw the prey. You have ideas, I expect?"

Gole nodded. That dark blot was waterproof canvas. It had been unfolded to reveal a pit in the soft ground roughly six feet wide and twelve feet long. Also, the enemy soldier nearest the pit was smaller than average, and wore something unusual on his head. Despite the long shadows and the weak candle-light, Gole recognized the Southie as Red Cap.

"You know the little one?" Nadros signed.

"Yes, that one is—"

"*Wrong.*" The sergeant chopped him off with a sudden, angry wave. "You do not know the little one. You do not have ideas. *You know nothing.* You can only guess, but you have nothing to guess with."

Gole clenched his teeth and closed his hands so he wouldn't reply.

Nadros signed, "Out here, one squeaker with a bad idea can kill the whole patrol. You will not think. You will not act. You will only watch and listen. Do not cost more lives."

This was Corphy all over again.

Gole nodded slowly, but his mind blazed with half-connected thoughts. Was every noncom a dimwit? Even worse—had the sergeant asked Gole a question simply to have an answer to reject? As many Tachba never bothered to think even two steps ahead, the premeditation of it stung worst. Next worst was seeing Grulle smirking in the background.

Sure, I'm new to the front, but this can't be how it works. This man was acting as if obstructing a replacement was more important than the enemy mere yards away. Was Gole *never* supposed to open his mouth? The Pollution in his deepest thoughts did make him yearn for simplicity, especially with an enemy so near. He wanted nothing but to receive clear orders, follow them, and know everything else was handled. But should he never announce the obvious? *Because it was obvious.*

The patrol was about to be tricked and destroyed. He didn't know how, only that it would happen.

THOUGH THE SERGEANT ALREADY SEEMED ANGRY, GOLE risked another question. "Still three there?"

Nadros checked again. "Yes. Three digging." He signed the word for 'nesting.'

"Three fingers of a five-fingered hand."

"I know, I know." Nadros scratched his chin. "We'll watch what they do next, and then take their weapons cache—"

Gole tugged the sergeant's sleeve. Nadros swung on him irritably. "Permission to guard the rear."

"Why?"

Gole shrugged. "Doesn't matter."

The sergeant frowned. "Are you...asking to hide?"

He'd expected Nadros to send him away in relief, but the man was going to make him sign it. Could nothing be easy? Gole flushed with humiliation and forced the word out: "Afraid."

"Afraid!" Nadros was astonished. "Is it fearful fear or madness fear?"

"A madness in me." Gole wanted to melt out of sight. At least his face was hidden by the blacking. "I fear I may fail at the wrong moment."

The sergeant leaned close, staring. The Pollution

discouraged lying, and it severely inhibited lying to superiors. There were always telltale signs when a Tachba tried to be false. Gole's hands trembled as he signed the words, but he wasn't lying, exactly. Every Tachba had some level of fear that their minds would fail at the wrong time. *And there's the Pollution again,* Gole thought sourly, *backfilling to make a lie into a truth.*

Nadros apparently found no dishonesty in Gole, but he remained suspicious. "Go, then. I can't stop you from having ideas, so your blood-fed will stay with me. He gets a bullet in the brain if you act without my permission."

Gole read the terse hand sign, his heart clutching. In fact, he intended nothing except to act without permission. He glanced at Grulle.

"Do not take fright, little flower," Grulle signed, in all seriousness. "I will keep you safe from here."

"Eyes wide," Gole signed, and slipped back into the darkness.

On his retreat through the patrol, Gole received several glances from the other boots.

"Orders," he signed, and that worked so well that he used it again when he circled around the squad. He was now acting without orders, but what else could he do? At least Pretty Polly was working to his advantage. His concern for Grulle faded the longer his brother was out of sight.

Gole moved fast, relying on the soft dirt to muffle his progress. In minutes, he was at the west-most edge of the patrol with nothing but emptiness in front of him. He stared into the night, wishing for more light. He could distinguish nothing except piles of dirt at odd elevations. Many of them looked like men hunched in greatcoats, a trick of the eyes. Some looked like crouching monsters. Before the Pollution could give him more enemies to fear, he took a deep breath and crept forward.

A southern hand squad would always number five men, though not always the same five. Those three Southies at the weapons cache meant there were two others unaccounted for.

They were trivially easy to find. Even Gole was surprised —and cautiously satisfied. *By my score, I haven't been wrong yet about anything on the eternal front.*

The two unaccounted Southies were crouching over another small wooden box a mere thirty yards from the others. The box was smaller than a regular munitions crate but just large enough to be ungainly, and it was heavy, based on how far it had sunk into the mumblety dirt. Again, some direct experience would have helped. Gole had no idea what the box might contain.

One of the enemy soldiers crouched over it, working a handle. *Winding?* It was a crank, but it didn't connect to any rope or chain. Only... When Gole looked closely at the disturbed earth next to them, he perceived two thin wires, nearly invisible in the dark. The wires started with the small crate and trailed into the darkness toward the weapons cache.

Gole knew what he was seeing.

They were charging a detonator. The buried munitions boxes weren't a weapons cache. Nadros's night patrol squad— and Grulle—had climbed a hill of frothy, insubstantial earth, and that hill sat on top of a pile of explosives.

❧ 13 ❧

Now the night made sense. The new scouting tape, which had given Sergeant Nadros such anxiety at the beginning of the patrol. The fact that the tape led them a new direction, away from the night patrol's familiar haunts. Maybe they hadn't interrupted the Southies, either...maybe the activity was part of it. To come upon Southies burying secrets between the lines—it practically demanded that Nadros hold fire and learn more.

Yes, it was patently a trap. Even worse, it was a trap that tweaked at the growing suspicions of the North. They'd been stung and bled by the South, and now here was what *looked* like a chance to be clever in return.

Gole's thoughts were still spinning when a small avalanche of dirt above the two Southies announced the arrival of more. Red Cap slid down the short slope, followed by the other two.

It was odd how Red Cap moved so slowly, with such care. Had he been wounded in the last encounter? His two much-larger squad mates were quicker. They used the innate Tachba ground-sense, flowing over the unpredictable earth like they were born to it.

The five of them gathered at the bottom of the shell hole like rocks sliding down a funnel. Red Cap was dwarfed by the other fingers of his hand—and that was odd too. As far as Gole had been taught, the South didn't tolerate that kind of variation, because of the unpredictable Pollution it brought with it. Anybody this far off the normal scale should have been hacked to pieces by civic-minded vigilantes, if they hadn't been smothered outright as newborn infants.

Gole jolted awake. *All five fingers of the hand squad are here.*

They had left the 'weapons cache' untended. This meant Nadros, the squad, and his brother might be creeping toward it right now...

A quiet voice in the still air. Gole couldn't make out the words, but the Southie working the crank started winding faster.

GOLE PUSHED HIMSELF OFF HIS PERCH, KICKING DIRT everywhere.

"It's a trap!" he cried. "Clear the ridge! Clear the hole!"

An angry exclamation from the Southies.

Gole dove away as a gun roared. The imprint where his body had been exploded as bullets punched through. The Southies were firing directly through the dirt itself, and it was so loose it provided no protection at all.

"That was the squeaker," came a voice from the darkness, one of the night patrol soldiers.

"Wandered off and woke the South," said another.

Gole moved again as another Southie fusillade sprayed the ground around him. They were shooting blind now, but that wouldn't last. When they got to the lip of the shell hole, he'd be an easy target.

"Into the pit, boys!" That was Sergeant Nadros's voice. "Grab what you can and fall back."

"No!" Gole screamed. He clawed back toward the night patrol, but the dirt was giving him no purchase. He would have run upright if he could gather his feet. The more he thrashed, the deeper he sank, the soil was like liquid. "It's a bomb! Get out of there!"

The detonator continued to crank with a steady whir. Soon it would have the power it needed to charge the wires.

Another volley of fire in Gole's direction.

Something hit Gole's head. His skull snapped to the side, cracking his spine. Hot fire poured down his neck and shoulders. The world went white with pain and he screamed.

"No, leave him there," came Nadros's voice. "He'll keep them busy—"

"Move, Grulle!" Gole sobbed. He lifted his head but it felt like granite, and his neck and shoulders were much too weak. Another gout of blood ran down his back. "Run!"

There was a fractional silence, empty of gunfire and Gole's screams. In the quiet, there was a calm order in a boy's voice: "Now."

The click of the detonator was so loud it could have been inside Gole's ear.

The earth in front of him geysered skyward. A wall of streaming sand intermixed with gobbets of flesh. Gole was prone, still trying to kick, and the main blast passed over his head.

He caught the other half of the explosion, which blew downward. It rocked the earth like the shrug of a giant and tossed him off the ground. He pin-wheeled into the air, over Red Cap and the detonator. For the briefest instant, perceptible only to his Tachba combat senses, he thought he saw their faces turned toward him. He went unconscious while still airborne and didn't feel himself land.

. . .

SOMEONE SHOUTED ABOVE GOLE. "I FOUND THE SQUEAKER, sleeping!"

"Bring him with you." The other voice sounded far away. It wasn't Sergeant Nadros but one of the others boots.

A hand closed on the collar of Gole's coat, not gentle at all. It pulled him without any seeming effort across the dirt. That was unfair—Gole had barely been able to move himself across the impossible mumblety dirt, so how was he being dragged?

"Your blood is everywhere, scrag." The voice held deep disgust. "Which you haven't even pinched the wound?"

"It's next on the list," Gole said, or tried to. At the first word, he coughed a solid tube of damp, corrupt soil onto his chest. It had filled his throat, which now felt coated with broken glass.

His convulsions started the wound again. He let run for a pulse or two, hoping it was washing clean of dirt, and then reached back with a hand to feel the damage.

His fingers sank into what felt like a *canyon*. The Southie slug had carved a ravine across the top of his spine, just below the skull. In the meat, he felt the hard knobs of exposed vertebrae.

"No," he gasped.

He wouldn't think about it. If he thought about the wound, he would surely lose his mind. He made his fingers explore it, losing and then finding it again as the soldier bounced him over the ground.

Gole located the narrowest side of the wound and pinched the skin. The flesh stuck together, but then snapped open at a particularly vicious yank of his collar. He closed it again, shifted his fingers, and pinched more of the wound closed.

The Pollution again, an adaptation for the battlefield. The first thing a soldier could try was to squeeze the wound closed. Sometimes it worked, but every man was different. Some Tachba could unaccountably snap back together from the most horrific butchering. *Maybe that's how Lieutenant Elyseuran survived his—*

"Which this ain't the cavalry, scrag," the voice snapped. "Do you have your feet back?"

The soldier didn't wait for an answer. He dropped Gole and dove away into cover, bringing his rifle up.

Gole turned his head carefully. The skin of his neck pulled tight all the way around, even under his chin. "What—*oh!*"

They were under fire.

They had been under fire all this time. Southie guns were going off, much too close, from the direction of his feet. Behind and beside him were the higher, faster cracks of Northern rifles. His squad, whatever remained of it, was fighting back.

Grogginess still fading, Gole tried to open his eyes—but they were already open. It was simply pitch dark at the moment. The smoke and falling dust of the explosion had vanquished all light. *How are we still fighting?* Gole wondered. If they were seeing what he was seeing, which was nothing—oh, they had the battle sense, of course. Shooting from intuition toward any sound in the din.

THE BOOT BESIDE HIM—WHO HAD SAVED HIS LIFE—shouted at him. "Perhaps a few bullets toward the enemy, squeaker?"

His rifle! *Crap.* His rifle, all this time, even when he was watching the Southies work the detonator...

For a bare moment, he pilloried himself as an idiot. He could have simply shot the hand squad, and maybe even hit a few before they returned fire. The unproductive sentiment washed away almost as soon as it arrived.

Pretty Polly at last! His battle sense, stunned silent by his wound and the explosion, finally reasserted itself. He flooded with guileless confidence. Faster reflexes, sharpened hearing —sharpened *everything.*

The limitless thrill of it.

In a blink, Gole was alert again. He sat up, groped around for any kind of cover, and slid into a shallow furrow in the ground. So he was Polluted, damn him and all the pains it brought, but this time he would use it. Maybe he was nothing but simple battlefield automation, bred to order for some long-ago race of foggy, tall creatures—it simply didn't matter in the grand scheme of things. What mattered was that he was tired of all this trickery. He knew what he had to do; he knew it with a clarity that surpassed his regular slow, stumbling thoughts. That tiny monstrosity, that aberration, that Red Cap bastard who moved like an old lady: Red Cap was going to answer for all of this.

He whipped his rifle off his back, where it had dragged in the dirt like an anchor and probably slowed the soldier saving him. In a fluid motion he separated the knot clasp and brought the rifle to bear between his feet. The movements were effortless, like a dream. He could even hear Red Cap scratching slowly through the soil. Gole could hear, *actually hear,* the deliberative shifts in the sand. Despite the gunfire, he could distinguish Red Cap's movements from the others.

The power of this! This freedom of action—maybe it was worth all the rest of the Pollution. If he could tap this power at will, he'd never use his brain again.

"Idiot, clear your—"

Gole heard the other soldier only after he pulled the trigger. The rifle barrel, packed with dirt, blocked the muzzle blast. The rifle exploded in his hands, flinging his arms open. It stomped him into the dirt like a train carriage landing on his chest.

Invincible Gole blinked out like a bad idea.

❧ 14 ❧

GOLE'S EARLIEST MEMORIES OF HIS HOUSE.

In the warm months of the year, the days filled with herding and farm work. As the house emptied before dawn, the youngest Tachba were collected in the kitchen and pinned to the floor with table and chair legs through their swaddling so they wouldn't be underfoot. There, the infants would watch the kitchen for hours at a time. The organized activity of the women was their first classroom. The children watched, learned, and developed until they were three years old if they were girls, and six if they were boys.

Gole's first specific memory was a table leg named Babaa, a particular best friend. His next memory was Orrie, one of his many older brothers.

Orrie was wild. He was nominally a *milk-fed*, supposedly more regulated than his blood-fed twin, but he had two helpings of the Pollution. Dizzyingly imbalanced, Orrie answered unheard voices and fell cheerfully into waking dreams. He made his family wonder what strange night-worlds he was seeing, even as he chatted and finished his daily chores.

Orrie wanted to speak to everyone and for some reason

he liked Gole best. He'd sit with Gole and Babaa between training sessions and explain the world beyond the kitchen table. It sounded fascinating! One lucky morning, Orrie even snuck him outside into the sunlight. The visual stimulation in the courtyard overwhelmed baby Gole and sent him catatonic. After that, whenever Orrie's wood-soled boots hit the kitchen floor, Gole kicked the air and squealed with excitement.

"You-hearing the boots, neh?" Orrie said once. "The boots making-your heart jump, my Best Little Bird?"

Gole stared back, struggling to form words and emitting nothing but drool.

"Well, Golephan, here is the story of the boots. They belonged to my older brother, whom we'll call Vavvie, but he tried to stab Papa so forget him. Before that, they belonged to Phaphta, who was found in the forest, in pieces. Before that, they were Papa's until they got too small. Before that, they were Papa's Papa's (who was strangled by Papa), and Papa's Papa's Papa before that. Can you believe that many Papas in a row? Momma, Gole *smiled!*"

Orrie tapped his heel on the floor. "These ancient boots! How many years will pass before one of us finds the patience to make another pair of boots this fine? It might be generations before the family spawns another obsessive cobbler—the Pollution mostly gives us fighters, doesn't it, Gole? We'll have to keep these boots going another century yet, my Best Little Bird."

True enough, the boots had next gone to Japha and then his blood-fed twin Phajaja. Then they'd been co-opted by a slight little girl—*Nana*. Nana was Gole's sister, older by two years, and in charge of educating him and his brothers. She had liked the boots' almost mystical power in the house: they were so storied that every male cringed when they heard them on the floor. They all had an association, some father or older brother who had worn the boots and meted out the training. She found them marvelous for keeping discipline.

As captivating as Orrie had been, Gole was days in noticing when the boy died. Even then, it was just a dim awareness of one voice less, one set of warm hands fewer.

It was Nana who told him the story, years afterward. Gole had mourned for only a moment before the Pollution swept through and erased the sadness.

What had happened was this: the older boys of the house had a pretend spear hunt going. It was another form of training meant to enhance task persistence. Hours of quiet stalking through the dark halls and rooms. The tension could grow unbearable, and when the Pollution's demands overwhelmed their young minds and sent them sideways into confusion or madness, they were beaten unconscious. In the next hunt, the boys would last much longer, because the Pollution wanted them to remain in the fight.

It didn't work for Orrie, though. He slipped out of conscious make-believe and into one of his dream-worlds. When Papa's man, Grueff, entered the main hall balancing a tremendous keg of beer on his shoulders, all the boys charged out of the gloom screaming like banshees. Only Orrie didn't turn his spear. He was wrapped in his dreams and oblivious to reality. He pinned Grueff against the door through his flabby gut.

Grueff gave a startled cry and dropped the keg. He reached up the spear's haft to catch Orrie just waking, and pulled the boy's arms off.

✣ 15 ✤

GOLE, THE VULNERABLE FOURTEEN-YEAR-OLD, BLINKED back into consciousness. He couldn't move his arms. He couldn't turn his head. His breath came in shallow gasps, but he couldn't hear them over the noise. He was being dragged again like a useless squeaker. He was not only failing to fight, he was actively keeping someone else from fighting. He tried to break free of the clutch on his collar, but what felt like a galvanic full-body wriggle didn't even register with the boot dragging him.

As he bounced along the ground—whoever had him was moving at a run—he generated a picture of the situation. It sounded like several things were going wrong at once.

Four breathless voices. Three rifles firing into the dark. The fourth rifle was quiet because its bearer was dragging him. This was a breakneck retreat under fire. Breakneck but orderly. The last remnant of the squad held onto its discipline with an iron grip, like a grenade that would kill everybody if the grip failed. They leapfrogged from hole to hole, providing covering fire. The resounding Southie rifles grew more distant with every volley. Nonetheless, a heavy slug took the tip off Gole's boot, missing his toes but wrenching his leg to the side.

He screamed, but it came out as a gurgle. If he felt enough pain, maybe Pretty Polly would come back, and maybe he'd be able to move himself.

"I don't know if I love you or hate you!" The soldier dragging him this time was not the same as the first. This one sounded almost cheerful. "Very kind in you to warn us about the big bomb at the start—a little late, maybe. On the other hand, you're like dragging an ammo cart with no wheels. You have a big dinner today?"

"Where?" Gole wheezed.

"We got turned around a bit. Now we're about three minutes away from the trench, and for me, four minutes away from a nap."

"I mean where is Grulle?"

"Ah, yes." The voice above him turned remorseful. "Which your blood-fed is dead, blown into the sky and fluttering down. I stepped on his corpse as we withdrew. He didn't respond, except to tell me to get off."

What does that mean? These impossible people. Gole said, "You're saying he's—"

"He was just dead-talking, I'm sure," the voice said. "You get a noise when you step on a dead one, but you know all about that, neh? Heard how you carry on with corpses."

"You get a noise if you step on live ones, too," Gole forced out.

"Well, true," the voice said, with sudden bafflement. "Damn my mind-meh, that's true at that. I should've thought it through. He was probably wounded."

"We have to get my brother!"

"No chance of that now. We're home safe. Grulle looked comfortable, if that helps."

The sky had grown faintly light but Gole, with his dirt-filmed eyes, didn't notice until the horizon wheeled above him.

He caught a glimpse of sandbags and landed at the bottom of the trench, unable to move.

Men were firing from the step-up, a new roar as they covered the last of the fleeing night patrol and chased the Southies back into the darkness.

Gole tried to grasp the wall so he could pull himself upright. His hand didn't obey. In fact, his arm was trapped beneath him, bent painfully behind his back.

He had just located and successfully moved his other arm when a face loomed over him.

It was Corphy, purple with hate. "Ye murdering scrag, what did you do? They say ye broke silence discipline. Now where is Sergeant Nadros? Where is the rest of the patrol? A write-off between the trenches, even your own blood-fed? You're getting your summary if I have to shoot you myself."

Gole had one arm he could move.

He swung at Corphy with all his focused might. It didn't work. He drew three bloody lines across Corphy's cheek with the stumps of his fingers.

He held his hand in front of his face and stared. The rifle, when it exploded, had taken pieces of his hand with it. He forced his eyes off the bloody mess and found Corphy, who seemed confused.

"I just punched you," Gole explained.

"Oh?" The lieutenant straightened, pulled his foot back, and kicked. The tip of his boot buried itself in Gole's ribs. Gole was fourteen, and Corphy was a grown Tachba with a full bloom of righteous anger. The kick emptied his lungs, lifted him off the trench gutter, and dashed him against the wall. Gole slid down it like a wet rag and found himself sitting miraculously upright against the sandbags. At least he didn't have to pull himself up now.

Gole couldn't savor it for long. Without air, his body gave up. He dropped unconscious again, this time definitively.

❧ IV ❧
GIVING UP

'Oggin Coe'   'Doggin Coe'

❧ 16 ❧

In which Gole Naremsa gives up, but sees a robot.

GOLE AWOKE TO VOICES, AND BECAME INSTANTLY ALERT. A Tachba voice he didn't recognize: "Which the squeaker saved a good many boots, ringing the bell on the Southies like he did."

"We don't know that, Sophalon." That was Corphy's voice. "All we know is that he lost silence discipline and the patrol turned into a bloodbath. Now I'm down ten boots and Sergeant Nadros. He was one of our best."

Corphy's tone was more modulated and controlled than usual, which Gole took to mean they were in the presence of a Haphan Overlord.

"He's awake," said Colonel Luscetian softly. Though the voice was lighter and higher than the Tachba, it cut through the discussion like a knife. "Golephan Naremsa, don't just lurk there playing dead."

Gole opened his eyes and saw he was back at HQ. It was

almost a repeat of the first day, only now it was Gole on the ground next to the map table.

He gathered his legs and stood. He'd been dragged on his heels, apparently, and for so long his boots were almost off. He stamped his feet back into place and swung his arms. He felt marvelously unremarkable. Almost fully restored, except that his neck was as stiff as a tree trunk and it crackled like stale bread when he moved it.

"Weren't you supposed to be wounded?" the colonel asked.

"Like I said, lazy." Corphy eyed him. "Sleeping and making the rest carry his weight."

Gole answered the Haphan. "Shot in the back of the head, colonel. Then the explosion flew me like a bird. Then my rifle exploded in my hands." He belatedly checked his hands again, spreading them open. The forefinger gone from both of them, and several more fingers with missing joints. The stumps had already scabbed over. He never used those parts much anyway, he decided, and recognized the Pollution at work in the thought. "The rifle was my fault. I didn't clear my piece."

"You seem to be thriving for someone shot in the back of the head," the colonel said.

After a moment, Gole realized this was a question in the Haphan style.

He turned to show them. The wound at the base of his skull felt rough and hot, but that could have been his decimated hands. He could tell, at least, that the skin was holding, which hopefully meant the damage would repair. The wound was a deep divot at the top of his neck, it would probably take weeks for the muscle to fill back in and his stiffness to vanish.

The boot next to Corphy, the one named Sophalon, laughed outright. "Which I give you joy in keeping your skull.

Looks like you almost had it off, Gole, and it's a vital part of one's person from what I've heard."

"Indeed," said the colonel. "The boy was not exaggerating. Shall we—*sir!*"

Gole turned to find them stiff at attention.

In front of them was a new Haphan, the smallest and oldest yet. He was unshaven and wearing an ill-fitting uniform. He was slovenly enough that if he had been a Tachba, he'd be marked for discipline and checked for madness. It was a moment before Gole distinguished the patch on the Haphan's breast and the black stars embroidered down his shoulders: an actual general!

"God, Luscetian, relax. You gave me a fright." The general looked them up and down, and then his eyes landed on Gole. However slovenly the rest of him appeared, the general's eyes were alert and quick. "What have I stumbled into?"

"General Tawarna," the colonel said, "just a minor disciplinary."

"La, I hate those." The general's gaze turned sad, pitying, and Gole burned with shame. "I wonder if this is the boot in question."

"Yes, sir, a new replacement, Golephan Naremsa."

The general glanced back. "Ah. The colonel learned his name."

The colonel smiled faintly. "I haven't been able to get away from him. He's been in the thick of everything since he showed up."

"Lieutenant," the general said next, and a tremor passed through Corphy's shoulders. "I wonder what this boot did, that I had to hear his name."

"Yes, sir," Corphy said stiffly.

"I rather meant to say, what did this boot do?"

"Do?" Corphy's ire welled to the surface. "Which first he kissed me one. Then wasting the lieutenant's time up until the lieutenant was plinked. Then breaking silence discipline to warn of an ambush. Then they tossed him back into the trench and he kissed me another one, or tried to!"

The general considered this, his eyes lingering on Corphy's face. The moment stretched long, until the Haphan's stillness was high contrast with the twitching and trembling of Corphy. They all sensed it, the fundamental difference between the two races. Gole couldn't help himself: he blushed with shame on Corphy's behalf.

"I wonder-meh, why I-walk the trenches at all," said the general. When he used the trench-talk phrasing, it didn't sound forced. "I only find new points of failure. Here, lieutenant, we have a story of failed discipline. When I hear that, I feel regret. Do you know that word? Regret?"

"Which I know it, my lord," Corphy mumbled.

"Yes, it's regret exactly. I see a boot brought up for discipline, and it's almost like I failed him myself. I failed him all the way until his last misstep. Have you ever felt that way?"

"No, sir."

"Never?"

"Well, maybe someday soon, if I'm lucky?" Corphy groped for more to say in the face of the general's silence. "Which our lieutenant were only just plinked, so I haven't earned my own regrets yet, you see."

"Oh, it's quite a thing to lead men, lieutenant." The general turned to Colonel Luscetian, who had gone still as a statue. Gole was unsettled to see that Luscetian's face was red, though he couldn't fathom why. "The feeling of it, all that pride in your men, and what they do, and how they act. It's tempered by the worry for them. Do you worry for your men, lieutenant?"

Corphy answered slowly. "I find it better if they worry about me."

"Ah, well, that part comes without effort." The general

shrugged. "Worry always flows upward, like it damn well should. We all worry what our superiors think, no? The magic happens when the worry flows downward as well. When the officer realizes, finally, that every damn thing that happens, good or bad, is an outcome they engineered."

The general turned fully to Gole, studying him up and down, but he still spoke to Corphy. "Lieutenant, we Haphans can't just shoot the bad elements. At least, we can't shoot them *here,* in the trench. If there is a problem and a soldier can't be redeemed, it must be fixed some other way."

"I understand, my lord," Corphy said.

"Good man." The general's eyes didn't leave Gole. "I understand how you understand me. Colonel?"

Colonel Luscetian swallowed. "Yes, my liege. I see the necessity."

Gole stared back. He'd have his chance next. They'd ask him to speak. *They had to.*

"Look how controlled he is," the general murmured, and shook his head. "Not even a twitch, and so young. I wonder how many we're wasting these days, eh, colonel?"

"Yes, my liege."

The general turned to leave.

Gole blurted, "But what about—"

"Shaxx!" the general snapped.

Gole's mouth snapped closed, almost making him bite his tongue. Corphy and Sophalon froze, their tweaks switched off like a light. The stop order, but in Tachbavim, and from the general himself.

"Do not add more regret to my day, son," the general said, and turned away. His retinue of Haphan officers, and a single ancient Tachba orderly, followed him around the traverse and out of sight.

17

"Good service, boys," said a new voice. "Return to your posts."

It wasn't Colonel Luscetian, who had gone still as only a Haphan could, staring after the general. The Tachba had waited in silence long after the stop order faded. Eventually, one of the other Haphan officers had stepped forward and dismissed them.

Corphy and Sophalon turned and disappeared down the trench.

"Yes? What?" the officer snapped, seeing Gole immobile.

"Am I really to have a summary?" Gole asked. He hated his voice, compared to the colonel's or even the general's. He didn't sound as he was, tired and angry and insulted. He sounded fourteen years old or younger. "The general didn't say it, but everybody heard it."

The officer glanced wryly at the colonel. "Caught at the last minute, Seul."

"He really can't shut up," the colonel said.

"You're speaking about me?" Fresh anger pulsed through Gole. "Maybe I'd shut up if I could get a clear answer."

The colonel's face turned hard. "Then it's a sad day, boot, because I won't be cornered by giving a clear answer to anything. I didn't think you were a child, but maybe I was wrong."

"My blood-fed is alive out there. My *brother.* I request permission to retrieve him."

"Denied."

"*Humbly* request permission."

"Denied."

Gole struggled for control. "If I'm to be executed, then nothing is lost if I don't come back. Surely that is obvious, sir."

"The cheek of this one!" This time, the other Haphan actually burst out laughing. Gole had never heard of an amused Overlord. It was unnerving, but Gole still wanted to punch him. Perhaps the Haphan noticed this because he said, "Oh, unclench your ass, Golephan. Stop making friends into enemies."

Stunned to silence, Gole watched the Haphan return to the map table under the awning.

"As for your summary, soldier," Colonel Luscetian continued, "I believe Lord General Duke Tawarna closed the book. Get back to your unit, that's an order, and don't give me another decision to regret."

A pinch of guilt. Gole dismissed that as the Pollution, his innate urge to obey authority and please his superiors. *I am manipulated inside and out.*

So he resisted, despite the unequivocal direct order. For resisting, he had yet another technique that had frustrated his sister Nana when he was young: he pictured long metal spikes through his heels, pinning him to the ground. The Pollution made his legs tremble but it couldn't move them, and without the movement, it couldn't convince him that obeying had been his idea all along.

Gole thought furiously, trying to ignore the Haphan's sudden interest.

This was the Haphan *colonel* in front of him. An Overlord. The last word on everything. To a Tachba facing the rest of his life on the eternal front, this Haphan was akin to a living god. When would he have another chance like this? Gole needed to squeeze every ounce of blood from this opportunity.

As it usually did when he needed it most, his mind failed to help. It veered instead to the skin sigil, the tattooed circle of leather he kept in his breast pocket.

His sister Nana, the little girl from his memories of faraway home, had been only two years older than him. Yet she'd been charged with teaching him and his brothers how to navigate the world. When she gave him the skin sigil on the day he was inducted into the army, she'd had such a proud, self-satisfied expression that he'd actually laughed at her.

Tachba boys hated their know-it-all sisters, hated and loved them. Even now, with Gole on the other side of the map and diligently trying to ruin his life, he couldn't escape her. Nana was telling him, as always: *Animals have feeling, people have thought.*

His sister would want him to be thoughtful. Between people, very little could be taken at face value. That sounded right to Gole—after all, what had he seen here? Corphy humbled without harshness. Colonel Luscetian somehow abraded by the general, without a single direct word. A random Haphan officer telling him to unclench his ass, as if they were friends with some affection... Yes, Gole was out of his depth, with no idea what he'd witnessed. At least, for once, he was aware of his lack of understanding.

Colonel Luscetian still waited in front of him. His eyes were over Gole's shoulder, focused in the distance. That was a

Tachba cue, something for a people easily mortified by what might be scrolling across their faces. It meant something like, "It's what you think it is, but I won't watch as you're humbled to realize it."

Had his thoughts played across his face? Had *Nana* been on his face, for all love? Gole wished again for the Haphan self-control. He'd master himself someday—if they gave him the chance—and become as inscrutable as the eternal front itself.

"Yes, of course, sir," Gole said evenly. "I will add no further to your regrets."

The colonel nodded, his face blank.

❧ 18 ❧

ON HIS WAY BACK TO HIS UNIT, GOLE MOVED THROUGH THE multiple lines of trench. They were as full as he'd ever seen them. Every unit had subtle variations that distinguished it from the others. The soldiers around him didn't wear rill helmets like his Fusiliers; instead they had forager caps. Also, their ammunition satchels had straps of braided twine rather than folded tarpaulin.

Their only similarity was in how they were engaged: sitting in rows and rocking, or staring at the sky with close-seeing eyes, or simply shaking their heads with their eyes closed. The Pollution strong in them.

He didn't know if this was normal in the trenches, or if he was simply more attuned to the symptoms at the moment. Either way, the other soldiers were collectively unnerving and Gole became aware he was muttering aloud. The accumulating stress and worry were undermining his control. He couldn't succumb, not yet.

Melt your teeth, Nana would say. For boys, the mind could be controlled through the body. Imagine a deed, and the mind will follow. Gole clenched his teeth and envisioned his molars melting together. His muttering stopped. One thing fixed.

He made unerring progress back to the 51st, despite the bustle and confusion of the trenches. Yes, he had grown all too familiar with the route to where the Haphan Overlords gathered to hear his latest failures. If he could have a day, just one, where he wasn't brought up for some transgression... well, then he'd have a day.

Don't get distracted, Nana said in his mind. *Tie Gole back to Gole's body. It's yours to command.*

GOLE PAUSED AT THE TRAVERSE WHERE THE TRENCH turned a right angle, and the 51st Ville Emsa Fusiliers took over. The edge picket, a soldier he didn't know, kept watch. The lookout shifted his weight from foot to foot and poked the sandbags with each finger in turn. Gole felt the urge to do the same.

No. More distraction. The Pollution seemed bent on turning him away from thoughtfulness. He had to *think.*

Gole would get his summary—Corphy would see to that. It would be unofficial, informal. Corphy would handle it inside his platoon. Thus, it would take place at the front before the unit was pulled off for rest leave. When it was done, the Haphans would be bothered no further with the regrettable story of Gole.

So—*think, Gole!*—if his fellow soldiers were going to kill him...it would have to be a quiet thing. Understood but not acknowledged. It wouldn't be in the open, subject to discussion. Gole would be struck from behind when the trench was quiet and empty. His watchfulness would lapse, and one of these twitchy, mumbling scrags would suddenly turn faultlessly competent and perform the one act at which all Tachba excelled. It would be fast and unexpected—except Gole now expected it and he would be alert. So it probably wouldn't be fast either.

Gole stepped up to the picket, who glanced at his unit patch before his face. "You found your home, the glorious 51st. There's nothing doing tonight. Unless the South has a notion to attack, we might even get some sleep."

"Did I miss the food?" Gole asked.

"Happily, yes," the lookout said. "Sadly, you might live longer having missed it. 'Twas boiled we-dunno-what that they poured into our helmets. The mess team called it *slosch*. We'em called it something else. You didn't miss a thing."

Gole almost grinned, but the soldier finally looked at his face.

"You're Gole Naremsa?"

"Am I?" Gole asked.

The soldier turned shifty. It was painful to watch. "I mean, la, what's your name, boot?"

Gole sighed. "Hello, my name is Gole Naremsa."

The soldier edged closer to him. "Hello, Gole. Did you just come from that direction?"

He pointed over Gole's shoulder, as if Gole would have come by any other route. As if Gole would actually turn his face away from the man.

"Yes, I came from that direction."

"How do you know?" the lookout asked, with unremitting cleverness. "How do you know where I'm pointing? Shouldn't you look where I'm pointing?"

"That depends." Gole permitted himself a tight grin. "What do you get if I turn around?"

It didn't occur to the soldier to even attempt to lie. "I get to hit you, for starters. Then another foul helmet of *slosch*. Then I'll get sent to hospital with *signed papers*. I'll be examined and then released for simple indolence, and thereby receive two extra days of rest leave."

The food and the additional rest leave sounded enticing even to Gole. He edged around the lookout, keeping him at a distance, until the other man finally understood that Gole hadn't been fooled.

"Well," the lookout said, "now you made this awkward."

"I think you helped a little, boot," Gole said.

After he passed the picket, the soldiers of the 51st became too numerous for any other covert attempts. Eyes touched him, left, then quickly returned. Conversations lagged as he walked past. He picked his way through one large cluster of soldiers still sipping *slosch* from their helmets.

"Make way," Gole cried out. "Gole Naremsa moving through. This is Gole Naremsa here, still alive. Gole Naremsa, you probably don't know me, but I have a beating heart."

It wasn't his intention, but the soldiers turned back to their food, ashamed. Gole nearly reached his home traverse, the one he'd shared with Grulle and really didn't have any reason to return to. That was when a corporal he didn't know called out to him.

"Scrag, attend me."

Gole waffled a moment, couldn't think of anything. "I give service."

The corporal was shorter than Gole and not much older, but like every other noncom he looked tough. Like he'd been fermented and cured on the front, with his softness burned away under fire.

"How can you give service when you're not even armed?" the corporal asked pointedly.

"Which my shooter exploded between the lines and I just made it back." Gole held up his hands, with their missing parts, but the corporal didn't spare them a glance.

"Facing the enemy unarmed is a discipline infraction."

"More than that," Gole said, "it probably slows down the war."

"Sarcasm?" The corporal crooked an eyebrow. "Sarcasm don't touch me."

"Then I know a boot you'd like," Gole shrugged.

"I don't follow joking much, either." The corporal pointed over Gole's shoulder, above the rear wall of the trench. Gole didn't turn. "For your infraction, you'll fetch an ammunition crate from the pile. They're in the explosives cache. The big crater, twenty yards toward the first support trench."

Gole presented his fingers again. "I will fumble whatever I carry. I'll take the night to let them heal. It would be bad service otherwise, and you might not get your box of ammunition."

The corporal dropped silent for a moment, actually stymied by Gole's answer. "Which the ammo don't matter, scrag. Screw your service, this is your discipline. Your discipline for wandering the trenches unarmed."

"If you give me a minute," Gole said, "I can think of a better punishment. Yours sounds lonely and a little dangerous—"

The corporal had him in the air before he could finish. He held Gole aloft one-handed by the collars of his coat. "Let me make it an order. Do you refuse an order?"

"You are unnaturally strong," Gole gasped.

The corporal's free hand balled into a fist and socked him in the ear. "Do you refuse an order, scrag?"

The world reeled in Gole's vision.

This is hopeless, Gole realized. *Screw being thoughtful.* Thinking only worked if other people were thinking too. Gole should have turned around when the lookout pointed over his shoulder. He should have taken the blow to the back of his head and been grateful for it. He should never have come to the front, not that he'd had a choice. He should have never been born.

"You know what, corporal?" Gole said, and his self control failed. Bitterness poured through the gap. "Fuck your order, it's stupid. Fuck this unit—from what I can tell, it's only good for getting killed. Fuck the whole war, you're all too dimwitted to fight it. And since you're letting me finish—*fuck you too.*"

From there, it was a simple matter of hanging in the air while the words penetrated the corporal's mind.

The first blow, to Gole's temple, snapped his head sideways. It was powerful enough to tear his neck wound open, but not to free him from the iron grip on his collar. The corporal hit him again as his head lolled, and after that, Gole lost count. It didn't matter, anyway. The bright impacts from each punch blended together.

He thought he felt lips and cheeks split open, but couldn't be sure. His flesh felt wet, and it could have been blood. The corporal dropped him to the trench floor—Gole was only aware of his limbs reconfiguring abruptly—but the man wasn't finished. A boot impacted his ribs, then his stomach. A heel stomped on one of his hands, flattening and spreading his knuckles.

THE BEATING ONLY STOPPED WHEN THE SOUTH intervened. A call to receive an assault passed down the trench line, putting the boots on alert. The corporal tore himself away and turned to the parapet. A few rounds came their way, and the 51st returned fire.

Gole fell unconscious.

When he woke again, the gunfire had increased. It may have been minutes or hours, but the corporal hadn't returned. There were fewer soldiers now in this length of trench, and they were shifting around the traverses on each end, perhaps to get better angles on the enemy.

A strange mechanical racket from the top of the trench... odd shadows in the blowing smoke. Gole tried to sit up but only managed to turn his head. He kept his eyes open through a feat of will and saw it, one of the marvelous Haphan beasts. A *bot*. It strode along the parapet not twenty feet from Gole, its massive blades spinning. It raised showers of dirt, and more: bits and pieces of bodies, old and new, flew into the air wherever the blades touched.

It moves with nothing moving it!

Though it was not alive, it moved thoughtfully and with care. It was a simple dumb contrivance, but somehow invested with agency and intent. This was Gole's first glimpse of true magic, his first sighting of something that matched the eternal front's renown. Gole forgot his pain and bitterness for a moment and watched with bald wonder. He stared until a turn of the trench took the bot away, and even its belches of steam faded from view.

It was walking so carefully. Gole's mind was placid and at peace, but only for a moment. Then: *Why is it here?* The bots were supposedly a last resort. *Are we being overrun?*

The Pollution pricked Gole's conscience. His unit was fighting without him. He tried to sit up again but dizziness knocked him flat. Gole had given up on the war, comprehensively given up, but Pretty Polly was still goading him to continue. His unit wanted nothing to do with him, and still he was almost shaking with the need to help them fight.

I'm no better than that Haphan bot. Gole was a simple dumb machine of bone and sinew, animated by the Pollution, and he moved with nothing moving him.

It's really everywhere, isn't it? There was really no escape from his mind. It really never ended, and it never would. If he'd had the means at that moment, Gole would have conducted his own summary personally, just to escape himself.

Instead, he slipped back to sleep.

When he woke next, the sky was dark. Moreover, the trench was empty and quiet. He was alone in the twenty-foot span. No one was visible even at the traverses where it turned. The other boots had drifted off or stolen away as Gole slept.

This is it, Gole thought. *I'm alone and I cannot move. What comes next...is the next thing.*

Underneath the blanket of aches that wrapped his body, a

spark of anticipation and interest. The Pollution, still guttering in his soul.

Gole heard a shuffle of steps nearby.

He raised a hand and croaked, "Over here. Murdering scrag over here."

The boots drew nearer.

"Hello, murdering scrag," said a voice Gole recognized.

Malley settled beside him with a maximum of disturbance and jostling.

Gole couldn't believe how much relief he felt. "Does this mean I'm sitting on Dephic again?"

He didn't wait for an answer, but fell fast asleep.

WHEN GOLE WOKE IT WAS DAYLIGHT. HE HAD SLEPT through the night and into the next day and somehow survived.

With calloused fingers on his forehead, Malley turned Gole's lips to a water skin and drizzled a few drops into his mouth. The moisture seemed to unlock a surge of strength, and he was able to speak.

"More water."

"It's water with blood mixed in. The soldier's antidote. Remember it for hangovers, too." Malley nodded at his leg. "Yours is right there."

A full water skin, bulging and damp, rested against his thigh.

"Where does the blood come from?"

"Ah, scrag, that's something you must never ask."

Gole shrugged and drank. The mixture was warm, with a distinct ferrous tang, but it spread quickly through his limbs. He drained half the skin and leaned against the trench wall with a sigh.

"Malley," he said presently, "I'm under a summary."

The old-timer was sprawled like Gole, looking almost as much like a corpse. He grinned without opening his eyes. "You don't say?"

"It's an *unofficial* summary," Gole amended. "The Haphans never ordered it, never said the word officially. We all heard it though. Corphy heard it."

"That's all that counts."

"Malley, has anybody ever survived something like this?"

Malley opened his eyes and looked Gole up and down before answering. "If you call this surviving, you have a generous soul. Anyway the answer is *no*. I've never seen a summary commuted once it gets rolling, and you're rolling like you started at the top of a mountain."

"Well, there it is," Gole said, trying to sound glum. The Pollution worked against him, tainting his mood with optimism. He was too frustrated to fight it. The frustration faded quickly, replaced with more optimism. It never ended: it never would.

"I've never seen someone survive a summary, but I've *heard* about it," Malley said. "It all centers on rest leave, when we pull out of the trench. That's when everything can be reset, so long as nobody presses the matter. Once the unit is off the line, the summary is the Haphan's business, and they have little stomach for it. There might be a transfer, and the condemned scrag at the root of the problem is sorted sideways to some other unit. The Haphans are too soft-hearted."

"Isn't it easier to simply do the execution?"

Malley shook his head. "Just like an official summary at the front will ruin the unit's morale, an official summary behind the lines ruins the Haphan's morale."

"We can't have that, can we?"

"That's right, get all your sarcasm out before Dephic

comes back." Malley smirked. "Dephic is hunting for your blood-fed, by the way. In case Grulle is lost or stuck between the lines. *That* boy is too good to waste."

Gole had a sudden, dizzying spurt of hope. "Grulle? You think he's alive?"

Malley shook his head.

"Could you be wrong?"

Malley shook his head again, but then shrugged. "Since your latest adventure, a few things have come to light. The tape that Sergeant Nadros followed for the night patrol, that wasn't *our* tape. It was a bunch of collected fragments, tied together. It wasn't *our* scouts what laid it out, it was the South being clever again. That added some weight to your version of the events."

"So the other soldiers believe me?"

"Of course they do, no matter what Corphy says. We all know he hates you. You're a master at spotting traps as far as everybody else is concerned."

"So the summary is off?"

"Of course not!" Malley chuckled. "A summary is a summary. Therefore, we want Grulle back with us. That way when you die we'll still have him, at least."

"But...I don't...None of that makes sense."

"You have some thoughtfulness to you, Gole. Maybe Grulle will also, after you die. He sees you plinked, there's a good chance he will bolt and turn normal. Maybe he'll start thinking complete thoughts at that point. It's very common in blood-feds, and wouldn't I know? I'm blood-fed myself. We need all the brains we can get, with South being so clever now."

"What..." Gole swallowed his frustration and tried for calm. "What if you idiots *don't* kill me, and you sip my wisdom straight from the source?"

Malley mulled this over as if were actually a new idea. "Wouldn't work."

"I disagree," Gole shot back. "And so does my valuable brain."

"I *know* you're confused, scrag." Malley sighed. "You're confused because you want everybody else to make perfect sense, even though we're all fighting madness just like you. The answer is utterly obvious, but only if you permit us to be flawed creatures."

"So explain, Malley."

"We Tachba can believe and feel at the same time. We can *believe* something is right, and *feel* something else is right—even if it's the complete opposite. On the one hand, we have wisdom received from our fellow boots, our officers, and the Haphans. On the other hand, there is the wisdom from our own minds and from Pretty Polly. Ask yourself, Gole, which of those two is more visceral to us? Which of those two is the bedrock?"

"First one, then the other," Gole sighed. "And then the reverse."

"Exactly. You're the same as the rest of us, Gole. I've seen you work against your own interests time and again."

"But I'm a dumb kid," Gole said. "I have an excuse."

"You're only dumb when it suits you. No, we all butt up against these little problems of the Pollution." Malley chuckled again. "You've simply elevated it to a new level."

"So I'm not under a summary, except I *am* under a summary. I'm right, but I'm not right. I'm clever, so you'll do away with me and hope to find my blood-fed."

"Now you're getting it."

Gole shook his head. "Malley, talking to you is an emotional journey."

The old-timer laughed outright. "You haven't heard the best part."

"What do you mean?" Gole went on guard again.

"Well, you slept peacefully through the night, didn't you? Your precious high-functioning brain doesn't have a bullet in it. The chance to kill you last night was forsaken."

An odd word to use, but he had a point. Gole said, "They had every chance to end it. Why didn't they?"

"Rest your mind. Those boots aren't killing you anymore."

"Why?" Gole pivoted back to him. "Malley, you *just* said the summary is a summary."

"The consensus is that *I* will kill you. Since you and I have had a few chats, it won't be as abrupt if it comes from me. It's often left to the friends to finish off a troublemaker, but you don't have any friends, so you know..."

"You're here to *kill* me?"

The old-timer met Gole's eyes. His expression was hard, and Gole belatedly saw the trenching shovel in his hand. One swat from that would cave in his skull.

"When you became my problem, Gole, I had to think it over." Malley let him hang a moment longer. "I decided you won't be killed. You'll get your chance to go on rest leave, and maybe you'll wriggle through. You're safe from all of us, starting now. Corphy be damned."

Gole waited for more, and nothing came. In the whole frustrating conversation, only the last part sounded definitive. If it was, then the death of an informal summary execution was no longer hanging over Gole. He was back to regular, trench-warfare death hanging over him, and a few days after that, a *formal* summary execution. It was strange how much relief Gole nonetheless felt.

"Malley, I'm glad to hear this news."

"I thought you would be." Malley closed his eyes again, and nestled down to nap.

Gole plucked the trench shovel out of Malley's hand.

The old-timer's eyes bolted open. "What the fu—"

Gole swung the shovel with both hands. He hit Malley's forehead and knocked him to the floor of the trench. Malley kicked once and went slack, still swearing even while unconscious.

.

V

RED CAP

❧ 20 ❧

In which Gole Naremsa finally learns wisdom.

THE ATTACK ON HIS FRIEND WAS WONDERFULLY BRACING—
or at least the Pollution thought so. With a burst of manic
energy, Gole vaulted directly to the top of the parapet, slap-
ping the sandbags with his hands and landing on his feet. He
was into the shell-pocked landscape and darting into the
darkness before he remembered he was still without a rifle or
any other weapon.

Too late to return now! He kept his eyes on the ground for
telltale signs of dead bodies and soon found some...north-
erners and southerners lying in strata, facing different directions. The weapons beside them were covered and clotted
with soil, and Gole passed them over. The last thing he
wanted was another explosion in his face, no matter how the
Pollution might juice him for it.

Finally, from a recent and not very stiff corpse he found a
boot sword, and inside the corpse's jacket was a double-

barreled pistol with one round. This area was a pillager's dream—he felt a tangible pull toward another cluster of bodies and whatever they might be hiding.

Instead, he cast about in the darkness until his hand found the scout's tape. Though it was obviously false—knotted links of irregular length—it was also clearly newer than the tape he'd followed with Sergeant Nadros two nights earlier. Also, this tape didn't have two days of dust, debris, and dirt covering it. In fact, if Gole had to guess, it had only been laid a few hours ago.

Perfect.

He gave it a shake and watched the tape undulate through the pock-marked landscape. As far as Gole could tell, the false tape went where he hoped it would, following a plausible path south. He trailed it, but not directly. He kept a dozen yards to the side. When he lost the tape in the falling darkness, he crept sideways until he found it again.

Each yard deeper into the darkness brought him closer to the waiting South. If they had laid this tape, as they clearly had, then he was closing on their next clever trap. Something was waiting for him out there—

Gole's hand fell on a living boot in the dark.

It jerked under his weight but didn't withdraw. Even as Gole registered the limb beneath him, his other hand arced in an overhead swing with the boot sword. He plunged it into the mass of the body—or he would have, but the stranger squirmed aside at the last moment. Gole's blade entered the soft dirt without resistance. Before he could pull back and stab again, the stranger rolled over it and trapped the blade, yanking the weapon out of Gole's three-fingered grasp.

Gole finally noticed something odd about his adversary. He scooted out of reach and said, "Why are you staked on the ground like drying meat?"

The figure stopped thrashing.

"Dancypants?" it asked.

For a full second, Gole swelled with relief. The Pollution may have minimized his concern, but it couldn't stop his joy when it unleashed.

"Grulle!" Gole launched onto his brother and hugged him. "I thought you were dead. Were you here the whole time, simply asleep?"

"Asleep!" Grulle laughed. "I disarmed you, and I am-tied to planet! What you-tied to?"

Gole tested the rope that had his brother spread-eagled on the ground. Like most things southern, it was irregular and imperfect but it accomplished the task, and there was a lot of it. The rope wound tightly around each of Grulle's limbs and stretched to four separate stakes. The stakes must have been of epic length to find any purchase in the soft dirt.

"I am surprised you couldn't squirm out of these," Gole muttered, trying to shift responsibility while he waited for an idea.

"Tied to planet!"

"Where is the boot sword?" Gole groped around his brother but couldn't find it. The earth in this area was strangely soft and loose, even for this sector. When he rose to his hands and knees he quickly sank into it. Gole could effortlessly reach into the soil to his elbows. He plumbed the area but still failed to find the blade. He felt deeper, and his fingers met a wooden surface.

He explored it by touch, wishing his hands were still whole. It felt like a lattice of crossed wood scraps, like a crate or a barrel had been broken to pieces. He knocked the wood with his knuckles, and the entire bed of soil under Grulle seemed to jump. Whatever was down there, it was big. Grulle had been staked out on top of something large that had been buried shallow.

"We have to get you out of here," Gole said, "but I can't find the boot sword."

"*My* boot sword," Grulle said. "Won it off ye."

"Well, I can't cut the ropes without it."

Grulle was unconcerned. "I will ask-meh for something sharp. When my friend comes back."

"Your friend, huh?"

"I can make friends, you scrag. Chatted all day with the Southies-geh, ere they-working."

Gole cast around in the soft earth again, hoping his hands would land on something that might cut the rope. A casing fragment, a bit of shrapnel, even a shard of bone. The problem with the interminable shelling, however, was that each explosion sent dirt into the air, and the larger debris settled lower. Like separating the wheat from the chaff, all the useful trinkets that Gole might have used had sifted year-over-year lower in the strata. After years of tilling from the artillery he had powder at the top and who-knew-what ten or more feet underneath. Probably a trove of interesting things.

"What were the Southies doing?"

"Fun tricks," Grulle snickered. "We'em should-stealing some of the good ideas, Gole. I thought them into my head so I can pull them out."

"Like what?"

"I forget." Grulle looked caught out. "Pull them out later."

"Doesn't matter." Gole spared a moment to pat Grulle's shoulder. "Besides, the last thing I need are more good ideas. Ask everybody who knows me in the war."

Gole shifted further away from his brother, probing the soft earth with his hands.

Grulle said, "My friend returning."

Gole froze. He heard it now, too. The stealthy thrush-thrush of a body squirming over the dirt. It was coming from the south. Gole nearly groaned with frustration. In this whole cursed world he had *four* ropes to cut and no way to cut them.

"I won't get you out in time," Gole finally admitted. "I must hide. Don't tell your friend about me, okay? Keep me as a surprise."

"Friend-meh likes surprise."

Gole pushed backwards, sweeping the dirt to obscure his prints. The oncoming sound was now just over the next crest of dirt, but he forced himself to be methodical and not make mistakes.

Gole had backed only halfway around a tall pile of dirt when Red Cap appeared beside Grulle.

Gole scrambled faster, right into the dirt pile—and delivered a powerful knock with his knee. He froze, waiting for it to cascade down and draw Red Cap's attention. *Damn this dirt for hating me.* But the pile, steep as it was, didn't collapse. Looking closer, Gole saw why. The pile was actually a cluster of corpses thrown together by chance artillery shell explosions—they wouldn't have died in that knot. Their limbs entwined and then spread like tree roots to give the pile structure. A group of bodies, knotted together like that, was called a 'corpse king.' In time, it would catch more bodies and grow quite large.

Red Cap's attention remained on Grulle, and Gole quietly pulled his limbs out of view. Then for good measure, he retreated another ten yards. He still had his brother in sight, but was distant enough that another trivial error wouldn't betray his presence.

When it came down to it, Gole reasoned, Grulle was probably safer from Red Cap than he was. This was yet another trap set by the South, and Grulle wouldn't be harmed until he could fulfill his role as bait.

Grulle said something to the Southie and laughed. Red

Cap whispered something back and lifted something in his hand.

Really? The Southie held something that looked like food. A rations tin, cut in half, with visible steam rising out of it. *Stew.*

Gole had grown up with veterans of the eternal front. The few that returned to the family were either too old to fight, or more typically disabled. The veterans had little to talk about except the war, and for those soldiers the war took place in the home trench and in episodes between fellow boots. The Southies were mentioned less in the stories than Gole had always wished.

Still, Gole had heard enough to know that the Southies were not vicious. They could be brutal and indifferent, but never merely cruel for the sake of cruelty. When they were called 'monsters' it was a joke, one the Haphans never understood. On the other hand, the Southies were never called kind. To see Red Cap treating Grulle with kindness was the last thing he expected.

For a moment, Gole stopped trying to plan and let his mind go quiet. The eternal front kept topping itself. Really, why train his ass off growing up, and why listen to war stories at all, if none of it translated to reality? Red Cap's strangeness didn't end at his size or his cleverness; there was now this *tenderness* to consider too. Gole watched the Southie hold the can to Grulle's lips and tip it into his mouth. Even as a captive of the South, the blood-fed was getting more food than Gole ever had.

He knew what he was supposed to do. He knew what Corphy would probably scream at him in this situation, and he knew what the Haphan Overlords generally advised when the enemy was in view. Gole had one round in a pistol, and he really should have killed Red Cap already. Moreover, there would be something on the man's body to cut the twine and free his brother.

Gole slowly drew his pistol. This time he checked it, and sure enough it had more of the omnipresent dirt clogging its barrel. He blew into the breach to clear it, then scooped more blockage out of the funnel-like muzzle with his longest remaining fingers.

Even when the pistol was clean and ready, he still hesitated. He didn't want to shoot, and at the moment it was his choice. He was in no present danger, and nothing in the environment promised death, pain, or similar other satisfaction that would trigger the Pollution. There was only food being shared, a kindness occurring.

Even better, he needed to confirm that Red Cap was indeed alone, and that the other fingers of his hand squad weren't lurking just out of sight. Gole only had a single round and he couldn't fight a whole squad. It was a plausible excuse, but Gole knew he was only waiting for more food to be put into his brother.

Red Cap and Grulle were whispering back and forth like old gossips when a chrysanthemum flare lit the sky. It bloomed with spears of light into a minor new sun, and sparkled as it floated on its parachute. Chrysanthemum flares were used by the North and they sometimes presaged an attack. On quiet nights like tonight, however, they usually indicated a bored northern Tachba, or a nervous Haphan line officer with "a feeling" about the looming darkness.

Grulle and Red Cap paused. The Southie turned to look at the new light.

There will never be a better chance.

Gole leveled his pistol at Red Cap—and froze.

Red Cap was female. The little Southie was a woman.

SHE CAN'T BE.

She really was. Tachba women only had a few years before they turned into child factories—that was the nature of their Pollution. The men had their carelessness, the women had endless cares. But for those first years of womanhood, they moved with matchless grace and beauty. They spoke with charming confidence and wisdom beyond their years. Even the Haphan Overlords weren't immune, if certain stories from history could be believed.

Red Cap was *definitively* female. The wide-set eyes, the full lips. Her jacket, bulging over her chest, now painfully obvious. A woman, a woman from the South, *fighting as a soldier.* In all his life—in all the training, the war stories, the whispered rumors—not a single word had ever included a woman.

Gole's hand froze first, and his pistol stopped moving. Then his whole body locked down like a stop order. It went against his very nature, against the built-in Pollution, to point a weapon at her.

Honestly, I must be hallucinating, Gole thought. Surely the Southies felt the same as in the North: that women are too few, too valuable, too *high function* compared to men, to spend in battle. When they weren't running households or outsmarting hordes of children, they were producing impulsive, violent new soldiers for the war.

Yet there she was. In the shifting light from the chrysanthemum flare, he studied her.

She was *much* smaller than him...if he laid his palms on her sharp cheek-bones, his hands would fully frame her face. Then, if he slid his hands around her head, his fingers brushing the brown hair tucked under her odd little cap, he would turn her face up to his. He would trace her narrow arched eyebrows with his thumbs. That smear of grime on her forehead—he would wipe it away, and she would blush at his attention. Those eyes, visibly green-brown even from ten yards away, would fasten on his. Beneath her small upturned nose, her full lips would part...

And then...well, if he felt her breath on his chin, it would be over, wouldn't it? Whatever part of him hadn't already melted from the blow-torch of her eyes would catch fire and collapse to the ground.

I'm losing it. Gole clenched his eyes and struggled for calm. *What's wrong with me?*

In his household, there had been a girl or two on the cusp of maturity, girls from other families. Prior to his induction into the army, he'd been mostly indifferent. Something had changed since then. Gole certainly wasn't indifferent now.

He also knew there was more than just *him* in his mind. The Pollution wanted more children for the war. The Pollution always wanted something. Of all the times for him to agree with the Pollution.

With his eyes closed, it was easier for Gole to structure

his thoughts. He pulled in the fragmentary clues and details since he'd arrived on the eternal front. The ones his mind had shied away from because they seemed to undercut what he'd expected the war to be.

Was it just this woman, a lone anomaly among the millions of Tachba on each side of the trenches? Had she alone created the sea change in this sector of the front, explaining the high attrition rate and the need for replacements in every unit? Did she explain the irritability of the officers who knew something—but not what—was changing their predictable trench war? Was it just her, or were there more?

With Red Cap, the enemy's clever new tactics suddenly made sense. The traps were about patience, about deferred reward. Difficult for Tachba men, trivial for women. Even worse, if one pretty girl could knock Gole over from ten yards away like some kind of puberty bomb, what would hundreds or thousands of them do to the eternal front?

The North would be in real trouble, wouldn't it?

Perhaps I shouldn't be squeezing my eyes shut with the enemy right in front of me, Gole thought. Because she *was* the enemy. Gole promised himself he would think clearly, and opened his eyes to the woman.

She was staring right at him.

He almost flinched, a movement she'd certainly see. After an anxious moment, Gole's eyes adjusted further and he saw she was staring past his position. She was watching the line of false tape which had led Gole to his brother.

Perhaps she'd seen something behind him, some movement? Maybe the shifting light from the chrysanthemum flare had cast a shadow that caught her attention. She hadn't picked Gole's face out of the jumble of sliding shadows, *yet.* He could delay taking action a few moments longer.

Red Cap turned back to Grulle. She leaned close and

whispered something into his ear, and then patted his shoulder. Envy pricked at Gole, but then faded as she collected her rifle and her satchel, looping them over her shoulders.

She was leaving and he was out of time. He had to kill her.

🦋 2 2 🦋

"IS THAT WHAT I THINK IT IS?"

Gole started at the soft voice by his shoulder and sank back into cover. Beside him was none other than Colonel Luscetian, the Haphan commander of the 51st Ville Emsa Fusiliers.

Forget how odd it was to see the colonel outside his regular environment, even though he had traded his pristine uniform for the dark green coat of a line soldier. This slow, weak Haphan officer had somehow crept up in the middle of a quiet battlefield without diverting a high-strung Tachba's attention. Gole had been precisely *that* absorbed by the woman—and that was the scale of the problem she represented.

"I've never heard of anything like this," Luscetian murmured.

More soundless movement in Gole's peripheral vision: Corphy. The lieutenant glanced over the ridge of dirt, absorbed the scene with Grulle and Red Cap, and lowered himself back down. Behind Corphy was Malley, sporting deeply bruised forehead. He winked at Gole.

It required no effort to reconstruct what had happened back in the trench. Corphy had found Malley unconscious and Gole missing. After that, one more report to the Haphan colonel about Gole's latest misjudgment. Then, for some reason, the colonel had assembled a squad of the 51st to make a sortie out of the trench. With the false tape to follow, it had been no effort to track Gole down.

"See, lieutenant?" Luscetian whispered to Corphy. "It wasn't so hard to find the Naremsa brothers after all. They're always up to something interesting, wherever they are."

Corphy glowered at Gole. "Which I believe it is time to start shooting."

The Haphan glanced at Red Cap. "That seems unlikely to me. Which of you is willing shoot a woman?"

Corphy shook his head.

Malley said, "It won't happen, sir. Shooting down a proper lady? So she's killed a few of us. Harmless fun."

"I know I'll miss the shot if I take it." The colonel turned to Corphy. "What do you suggest, lieutenant?"

Corphy searched his mind. "We watch and learn."

"Maybe your squeaker has one of his brilliant ideas?"

For this, the lieutenant had a ready answer. "Which I think we've had enough of his brilliant ideas."

The colonel finally turned to Gole. "Speak."

"Stop using tape for soldiers to follow between the trenches," Gole said. "I can't imagine a worse idea now that the South knows about tape."

"Agreed," the colonel said. "But what about the—the little Southie?"

"For her..." Gole sighed. He couldn't put it off any longer. "Someone who doesn't know she's female."

"Precisely," Luscetian said. "Corphy, who is watching our six? Get them up here."

The word was passed with hand sign, and soon a new

soldier crawled up. He looked even younger and greener than Gole, but at least he had a rifle, and it was clear of dirt and ready for use.

The colonel pointed at Red Cap. She was squirming up the slope and would be gone from sight in only a few seconds. "Emperor's service, soldier. Shoot me that man in the red cap."

The boot rose to one knee and smoothly brought his rifle to his shoulder.

A deafening crack. Red Cap arched backwards. Another shot, and the figure spun to the ground next to Grulle, not moving.

"That will draw some attention," the colonel said. "Naremsa, go collect your brother before the snipers start up."

"Yes, sir." Gole moved to obey, then hesitated. "I, uh..."

"Let me guess," Corphy said, "you're missing a vital piece of equipment?"

Malley *tsked* and passed him a trench knife.

"You have three ticks of the clock, soldier," the colonel told him.

STILL TIED TO THE GROUND, GRULLE WATCHED GOLE'S approach with calm, alert interest. "Gunfire. Little friend-meh goan' shot."

The woman with the Red Cap lay next to Grulle, three feet away, not moving. Gole glanced at her, then looked again.

She was alive.

Her body was contorted and her limbs were askew, but she was blinking. Her breath stirred the powdery dirt under her cheek.

Gole couldn't see where the bullets had struck her, and there wasn't much blood. Perhaps she wanted to play dead so they'd stop shooting. Up close, however, she was obviously alive. So: she was too wounded to feign death, but perhaps not too wounded to survive.

"Turns out she's a girl," Grulle added.

With four quick movements, Gole cut his brother finally free. Grulle sat up and rotated his wrists. "Which it hurts getting my fingers back! Not the feet-meh. Wait... yes. Feet-meh hurting too."

"Hush, Grulle," he said. "There may be more of them around."

He turned back to Red Cap. She watched him with pene-trating eyes. The chrysanthemum flare had sputtered out minutes ago and it was again too dark to see the green in them.

"For your kindness to my brother," Gole whispered, "I'll treat you like you're dead."

She didn't answer.

"I'm sorry about this next part," Gole added.

And he was. For anyone watching, Gole had to make a show of searching Red Cap's body. She still didn't react, except to release a sigh of dismay as he knelt over her. Tears ran in tracks down her muddy face, but that was pain and not fear. Blood finally started to show through her coat. Its slow arrival was itself a positive sign.

He turned self-conscious as he unbuttoned her coat, and then several of the buttons of the odd, unmilitary linen blouse beneath. *There she is, then.* His first nearly naked woman of child-bearing age.

"Throughfer under your ribs on your left," he reported tightly. "Get some pressure on it. It's bleeding but not mortal in itself."

"Yeah," she said. She gasped as he tipped her over.

"A crease over your spine near your ass. No blood. Can you move your legs?"

"Feeling is coming back to them," she said.

"Mine too," Grulle put in.

Because he'd be asked about it, Gole rifled her coat. A metal pen, a tiny notebook, and a pair of occlusors for measuring artillery trajectories—these went into his pocket as found battlefield intelligence. Another item, a stiff paper card, puzzled him. It wasn't writing and it wasn't a map, but one side had a swirl of black lines jumbled together. Some of the lines were feathered, as if to make shading.

"A picture of my papa," Red Cap said softly.

"This? It's a mess."

A low, throaty laugh, followed by a catch of pain. "La-meh, I know it is. Drew it himself, so me-remembering him."

Gole shoved it back into her coat. "When you can move again, go back to your trench for help. I can't do more for you. I probably wouldn't if I could."

She nodded. "The war and all."

"I don't know how quickly women heal; it's never come up. If you were a male, this would already be sorted."

"La," she whispered. "The story of my life."

Gole hesitated. "Tell me. Are there many more like you on the front? More women?"

As he expected, she didn't answer the question. She did give him something else. "'Ere the sun is-climbing, Northie, the snipers then will-come. A holiday festival of snipers, la. Ye must be safe, and go."

"Thank you," Gole said.

"Kindness spurs kindness."

They heard a soft whistle, far away. Colonel Luscetian's patrol had moved out, and was making good time by the sound of it.

Gole shook himself out of the strange moment. "Grulle, we're leaving."

"Bye, pretty girl." Grulle darted away without a backward glance.

Gole saw the expression on her face. "There's more he can't say. He'll think of it later and want to tell you."

"You-telling him back for me."

Gole nodded. When he turned to leave, she added, "Wait! Button me up at least."

Gole closed her blouse, fumbling the buttons under her excruciatingly close and unwavering gaze. He tried to think of something impressive to say about his missing fingers and gave up.

When she was covered, he still wanted to do nothing but stare at her. He closed her jacket for good measure. He told himself he was only being kind, not drawing out the moment.

"I think," Gole said, "you could have worked these buttons faster than me."

Something shifted in her expression. He couldn't be sure through the grime, but she might have been smirking at his discomfort.

She said, and he would never forget her voice: "I liked your way better."

❧ 23 ❧

GOLE CRAWLED MECHANICALLY THROUGH THE DIRT, ARM over arm, following the patrol. Thanks to the false tape and the fresh prints on the ground he had little chance of getting lost. And lucky for that, because his mind was still with Red Cap. Her pout when Grulle left...and her teasing when she said those last words...*were girls magical?*

Gole also remembered the colonel's eyes. They had not dwelt on Red Cap, either before or after she'd been gunned down. The colonel had been memorizing the area, noting landmarks. The Haphans would return as soon as possible, this time without their servitor Tachba, to collect her body. It was the only plausible next step. The Haphans would want physical evidence of this major change from the South. Even as only a corpse, she was too important to the empire and the war to leave on the field.

Gole hesitated. *Will she live? Will she be able to move in time?* He didn't want to ruin the whole war, but he did want her to survive. He wanted her to remember him, maybe.

· · ·

"A LITTLE CLEVERNESS WOULD SERVE NOW," MALLEY SAID from beneath him. "This is becoming a habit with you."

Gole looked down. He had, yet again, crawled on top of somebody. He shifted to the side, and found himself back with the patrol.

"Head down, idiot," Corphy snapped from behind him. "Can't you hear the snipers? Your skull don't matter none, but you'll draw their eyes to the colonel."

Gole glanced the other way and saw that the Haphan was still with them. Now that he listened for it, Gole could also hear the remote pip-growl of Southie sniper rifles. Their reports were numerous and persistent, nearly the only sound on the battlefield at the moment. If Red Cap had managed to spring her Grulle-baited trap on a northern patrol, the ensuing confusion and casualties would have turned it into a monumental loss for the North.

"Soldier," Colonel Luscetian said to Malley, "check our path home and confirm the way is clear."

Malley nodded and clambered out of sight. Gole was alone with his lieutenant and the colonel.

Corphy said, "Which we should move too. The sun is in the air and we're in the open. La, it was a bad idea to wait for the squeaker. No criticism intended."

When the colonel didn't immediately answer, Gole and Corphy turned to him.

"Tell me, lieutenant," the colonel said quietly. "Do you still believe Gole deserves his summary execution?"

Corphy barely glanced at Gole. "By this point, sir, I'd say he deserves two of them."

"Are you certain, Corphor?" The colonel went very still. "After what he discovered, after what he's shown he can do in these few days? He is a magnet for trouble. There's more than a little promise there."

The lieutenant shook his head. "He only promises to

break more rules. Haphan rules, if I may point out. *Your rules.* This scrag thinks he's clever, but he's a danger to himself and others. I only wish we could have our Summaries at the front, as a message for every new squeaker who stands up and thinks he's special."

"Well, there it is." The colonel met Gole's eyes, his expression opaque. "The war is changing and the rules must change with it. As it turns out, lieutenant, we Haphans *can* conduct a summary at the front."

Before either Gole or Corphy could react, the Haphan climbed to his knees. He rose into the open air, the sunlight slanting across his grim face. Colonel Luscetian was fully exposed from the waist up.

"Sir!" Corphy lurched upright to drag him back down. "The snipers!"

Luscetian snapped a salute at his lieutenant.

Corphy's hand raised reflexively to return the salute, but paused halfway up. Realization unfurled across his face—then his neck exploded. A sniper round through the top of his spine. He fell sideways, his head spinning on a single remaining tendon.

Luscetian dropped back into cover at the same time, untouched. He hugged the ground as if it was home, blinking in the dirt with his face half buried. He stared at Corphy's head, with its eyes that turned his direction and then slowly closed.

Gole's heart thudded in his ear. When he found his voice, he said, "You're alive and well, sir."

"So I seem," the colonel said. He wrested his gaze away from Corphy. "I seem to be unmarked."

The Haphan's tone was strange. Gole searched the colonel's face, and found himself being closely studied in turn. Was the Haphan checking Gole for madness, assessing his fitness for duty? *He would only do that if he thought I was shaken by something I'd seen.* Did the colonel suspect he knew? *How in hell could I not know?*

"That..." The Haphan faltered, then tried again. "That may have been an error of trench craft on my part."

Gole understood, then. His answer would decide what happened next. He said, "The Haphans never err, sir."

The words seemed to make the colonel more wretched, but he nodded. "Of course we err, Gole, but it's not a common topic of conversation."

"It's never been uttered in my hearing, sir," Gole said. "I don't expect it ever will be."

The colonel finally broke eye contact. "Someday we might deserve that confidence. Anyway, well spoken. A clever soldier to fight our clever new enemy. May you be the first of many."

Malley burst back upon them, making them jump. The old-timer's frilled helmet was fully missing, and he had several new bullet wounds at the tops of his shoulders, still pulsing blood.

"The way is clear, sir," he reported. "Don't judge by my looks, it's mostly safe and quite exciting." Malley noticed Corphy's body between them. "I daresay it's safer than here."

Colonel Luscetian nodded. He was back under control, his face again impassive. "Good service, soldier. But in case I do get plinked, let me tell you that this man"—he pointed at Gole—"is out of his summary, informal or not. The Haphan Empire expects great things from Golephan Naremsa, and only the enemy has our permission to harm him now."

Gole burned with relief as Malley's eyes raked suspiciously between them.

"Yes, sir," Malley said, and then he grinned. "Though his blood-fed will probably be disappointed."

"Also," the colonel continued, "while Gole prepares to do his great things, perhaps you can teach him some basic trench craft. Like bringing weapons on patrol. Knives for cutting ropes. The like."

Malley smirked. "La, sir! On the eternal front, all things are possible."

With that, he turned and led them safely back home.

The End

ABOUT THE AUTHOR

Walter Blaire is the author of the *Lines of Thunder* series of books, about the Haphans, the Tachba, and the interstellar CivGov. The full series is expected to be five novels when complete, with a collection of short stories and short novels as side trips.

If you enjoyed this book, look at the other stories set in the same universe, available at a fine online bookstore near you.

Keep track of the Lines of Thunder universe at:
www.WalterBlaire.com
walter@walterblaire.com